KOKILA

An imprint of Penguin Random House LLC, New York

First published in the United States of America by Kokila,
an imprint of Penguin Random House LLC, 2023

Visit us online at PenguinRandomHouse.com.

Library of Congress Cataloging-in-Publication Data
Names: Rivera, Lilliam, author. Title: Barely floating / by Lilliam Rivera. Description: New York: Kokila, [2023] |
Audience: Ages 9–12. | Audience: Grades 4–6. | Summary: Twelve-year-old Natalia's dream of becoming a
synchronized swimmer is in jeopardy when her parents decide they are against a sport that emphasizes looks,
but Nat is determined to change their minds. | Identifiers: LCCN 2022048289 (print) | LCCN 2022048290 (ebook) |
ISBN 9780593323120 (hardcover) | ISBN 9780593323144 (ebook) |Subjects: CYAC: Family life—Fiction. |
Friendship—Fiction. | Secrets—Fiction. | Self-esteem—Fiction. | Synchronized swimming—Fiction. |
Mexican Americans—Fiction. | Classification: LCC PZ7.1.R5765 Bar 2023 (print) | LCC PZ7.1.R5765 (ebook) |
DDC [Fic]—dc23 LC record available at https://lccn.loc.gov/2022048289
LC ebook record available at https://lccn.loc.gov/2022048290.

Printed in the United States of America

ISBN 9780593323120
1st Printing
LSCH

This book was edited by Namrata Tripathi, copyedited by Debra DeFord-Minerva,
proofread by Jacqueline Hornberger, and designed by Asiya Ahmed. The production was
supervised by Tabitha Dulla, Nicole Kiser, Ariela Rudy Zaltzman, and Hansini Weedagama.
Text set in Utopia.

BARELY
FLOATING

LILLIAM RIVERA

Kokila

To my synchro water baby, Isabelle

CHAPTER 1

~~~~~~~~~~~~~~~~~~~~~~~~

It's 10:30 in the morning, and Roosevelt Pool is packed with people. Big kids. Skinny kids. Babies shrieking because of the cold water while mommies try soothing them with sweet baby talk. Rough kids dunking each other. Girls in long T-shirts, hiding their panzas. Abuelitas sitting on the pool steps, cooling off their wrinkly legs.

Then there's me.

I'm at the far end of the pool. The deep end. That's where the real action is. I'm about to take Beto down. He doesn't know this, of course. Just look at his clueless face, staring out at nothing. Beto is all cheeks, like a chipmunk storing food or like Kiko from that old *El Chavo* cartoon. I'm about to deflate those cachetes with pure muscle. What does El Chavo always say? Beto didn't count on my astucias.

"Hey, Beto, I bet you ten bucks you can't beat me in a race across the length of the pool." My voice is loud enough so that everyone can hear. Beto turns to his group of friends and shakes his head.

"Dude, your sister," he says to Ramón. He laughs off my challenge.

"Nat's not playing," Ramón says. "She means business."

There are three boys in my family: Ramón is the youngest. Julio, the oldest, is married with a kid on the way. And Raymundo is attending college in Santa Barbara. Ramón is in high school, and so is his ugly friend Beto. Beto is on the water polo team. I'm not on any team. I'm just here to make money.

"Ten bucks says you can't beat me."

I lean back against the pool deck. Those around me chuckle or shake their heads.

"Why can't you just chill for once?" Sheila says.

Sheila is my cousin. Technically, Sheila and Ramón are supposed to be taking care of me. "Taking care," however, is forever in air quotes. It's hard to contain a person like me—especially when that person grew up in a house full of stinky, loud boys. Sheila doesn't get it. She's an only child who loves clothes and Fenty lipstick.

"Me and you, swimming across the pool," I repeat. "You know how to swim, right?"

Last week, I made an even twenty bucks outswimming twins. The twins were running their mouths about how there was no way a gorda could swim the full length of a pool. There's always someone underestimating me. They see my stomach rolls and think, *She can't possibly be physically fit.* When I emerged victorious, the twins had no choice but to pay.

Beto looks nervous. If he doesn't take the bet, he's a punk. If Beto agrees to race me and I end up beating him, which I will, what does that make him? So much is weighing on those balloony cheeks.

"From here to the other end of the pool," I say. "C'mon. What are you afraid of?"

The crowd around us grows. I look over at my best friend, Joanne, who sits in our shaded spot reading *Summer Hero*, volume two of the manga series Kurahashi. I haven't had a chance to read that one yet. I always get the manga after Joanne finishes, and then we dissect every little detail in the story. Joanne shields her eyes now and gives me a timid wave.

"Fine, but I'm only doing this to teach you a lesson," Beto finally says.

Teach me a lesson? Even Ramón laughs at this statement. Beto hasn't been around my house much, nor around me. He doesn't understand that I'm like a shark: relentless. When I was seven, I sold chicles to the kids in my class until another mom told my mom. At ten years old, I found a way to teach kids curse words in different languages. A dollar a curse word. That lasted for a couple of weeks. Now that I'm twelve, I understand the importance of using my skills. I'm fast. I can beat anyone in this pool if I set my mind to it.

Sheila tries to be the timer. No way. I don't trust her. Besides, it's not a good look for family to be involved in business. Instead, I hand the honors to a boy with shaggy curly curls covering most of his face. He parts his hair away from his big eyes. Good. He'll do.

"On your mark," Shaggy Boy says.

Kids slap my shoulders. Girls giggle. Some of them think I'm cool to do this. Others think I'm too much. I'm not doing this to please anyone. I'm doing it because I can beat Beto.

I pull down my goggles.

"Get set."

One more glance at Beto. He's laughing. He thinks this is a joke. I'm going to win.

"Go!"

I propel my legs against the wall and shoot out like a rocket. The start is the most important part of any race. I glide underwater for as long as I can until I have to break the surface for air. Professional swimmers always do that. One quick gulp of air and I turn to Beto. He's ahead, but not by much.

Okay, time to catch up.

My arms are like octopus tentacles, stretching as far as they can. I scoop water and direct it behind me. I kick my legs hard. Every stroke is important.

In this pool, I'm a swordfish. I'm a mermaid. I'm an underwater speed demon.

And this demon is about to take Beto down. Too bad, so sad.

A quick look. Beto is slowing down. He's about to get beat by this twelve-year-old. Where has his training from water polo gone? He finally notices me. We are neck to neck. I bet anything there's fear in Beto's eyes. I dig deep and find the last burst of energy to seal this deal.

And *boom*!

I tap the end of the pool. Beto pulls in seconds later. The crowd around me cheers. I never get tired of this, the part when I'm victorious, when I'm able to prove the haters wrong. "Never underestimate the power of a Latina"—that's what Mom always says. Dudes are always trying.

Poor Beto. He's breathless, practically hyperventilating.

"I won!" I jump out of the water and point to my empty palm. "Pay me!"

"No way," Beto says, pushing my hand away. He's barely able to form words. "I'm not paying you."

"Pay me! I beat you." I don't like where this is going. If you lose, you have to be a good sport. Besides, this is business. "Everyone here is my witness. I beat you fair and square."

Beto tries to brush me off. The crowd eggs him on. They call him weak. *How could you let a kid beat you? You let a girl win.* I don't care if he's in his feelings right now. I won without any tricks. It was just me in the water.

"You owe me ten bucks," I say. "Give me my money."

Beto and my brother walk over to where Sheila and her friends hang out. They try to ignore me. I will not let up. Beto can't renege on this deal.

"I'm not leaving until I get my payment." I stand in the middle of their group, right on some girl's towel. I'm a Taurus, and we're known for our willingness to get into people's faces. I will not move from this spot until Beto places some crisp bills on my hand. The girls complain about me standing on their towel. Beto pleads to my brother.

"That's enough, Nat," Ramón says. Not even my own blood is willing to back me up. Honestly, what's the point of having brothers when they won't stand up for what's right?

"Go play with your friends," he says.

"No," I say.

If Ramón won't help me, then I'll have to get ugly. I jump on Beto. "You owe me."

Beto doesn't know what to do. He knows well enough not to hit me, but he also doesn't want his eyes scratched out. So there is a whole lot of awkward wrestling going on.

"Give me my money!" I yell. Beto is obviously stronger, but like I said, I'm a shark. I will not stop.

"You have an interesting sister," I overhear a girl say to Ramón.

I peel myself off Beto and turn to face the girl. "Well,

you have an interesting *face*," I yell. If she wants in on this, I will gladly include her. Before I can jump her, my brother pushes me away from the group.

"Go away, Nat." Ramón has Mom's face. The serious, not-in-the-mood-for-this face. I head to Joanne, who places an arm around my shoulder.

"I can't believe it!" I say. I'm so angry.

"You can't win them all," Joanne says. She tries her best to protect her manga from getting wet.

"Of course I can," I say. "Mom says if I work hard enough, I can do and be whatever I want. Beating Beto was just a tiny part of today's goal. Besides, if I don't get paid, then everyone else will think they can do the same. Know what I mean?"

Joanne gives a slight nod.

"Sure, but there will be other chances to make money," she says.

I love Joanne, but honestly, I wish she could see things from my point of view. Joanne doesn't like confrontation, which is funny because confrontation is basically how we met. It was in first grade at Sagrado Corazón Elementary School. A sweaty boy in our class kept pulling Joanne's hair. The teacher did nothing. Instead, Ms. Castro said this weird thing to Joanne, "He probably likes you." I couldn't stop thinking how Mom says, "Your body, your permission." So when the boy decided to touch Joanne's hair, I grabbed *his* hair and wouldn't let go. Mom was

7

called in. The incident brought a quick end to my Catholic school days. It was worth it.

Joanne eventually ended up in the same middle school as me, and we've been best friends ever since. I'm always ready to defend us no matter what, while Joanne would rather hide behind a book and wait things out. Somehow, the relationship works.

"We don't need Beto," Joanne says. "We have more than enough money."

It's true. I'm saving money so we can go to the big anime con on October 30. For the past two years, Joanne and I have attended and cosplayed our favorite characters. Because Joanne's parents don't believe in spending money on "dumb" stuff, I save enough for both of our badges.

"I want to make sure we can buy cool manga at the con," I say. "Beto's going to pay. I just have to figure out how."

"Oh, here you go." Joanne digs through her tote and pulls out a brown paper bag. She hands the bag to me.

"Yes! You remembered!" I give Joanne a side hug and quickly pull out the latest issue of *Vogue*. Although my fingers are dry, I still wipe them off on the towel, just in case. Manga is really Joanne's scene. I just like the cosplay because I get to wear awesome costumes and makeup, which Mom only allows for the con. Mom thinks girls don't need to wear makeup to feel empowered. It's the reason why I hide the *Vogue* and *Elle* magazines I ask Joanne to buy for me. Mom hates those things. She thinks they add to self-esteem issues and a "distorted view of the body."

I get what she means. I do. I wish Mom could be more understanding. Every time I try to state why I love makeup and fashion, she shuts me down with big words and statistics. She's really good at winning arguments. It's hard living in a house where you have to outsmart the smartest woman on earth. I really just like the pictures.

I can't wait to go through this issue. I'm starting to feel a little bit better. Joanne returns to her reading, and I try my best to concentrate on the fashion candy before me. I hear Beto's cackle. He needs to pay. It's not over until I say it is.

Christian, the pool manager, interrupts my scheming. "Everyone, we have a special treat today. The city's only Black-owned synchronized swimming team is here to give a short demonstration."

"Synchronized swimming," I say loudly. "What's that?"

"Just you wait," Christian says.

The pool-goers are reluctant to get out of the deep end, but they eventually do. A group of six swimmers wearing matching electric-blue swimsuits march across the deck like soldiers. The swimmers are all different shapes and sizes. They look older, like high schoolers, but there's one who looks about my age.

Christian gives a thumbs-up, and music starts to play. It's Beyoncé's "Break My Soul." Then the swimmers do the wildest thing: They jump into the water and start to dance. Actually dance. Hands up in the air. Wrists snapping. One swimmer lifts another by the waist. The swimmer who is lifted waves to the crowd like no big deal. There are more twirls and leg lifts and all kinds of cool movements timed to the song. I can't believe it!

The crowd claps and sings along. The swimmers all go underwater and kick their legs straight up at the same time. Heads turn to the left, then to the right. The music reaches its climax and the swimmers dive deep into the water. There's no sign of them. It seems like we are all holding our breath in anticipation. I know I am. Then she pops up. A sole swimmer, standing on the shoulders of another. She's the one who looks my age, and here she is being lifted up high. As if that's not amazing enough, she smiles before doing a flip in the air. A FLIP!

In all my twelve years of life, I've never seen anything like this. Ever.

"Wow," I say.

"Wow," Joanne says.

The swimmers pull themselves out of the pool and then stick their hands up at the same time and wave. One of them addresses the crowd.

"Hi, my name is Yvette, and I am part of the L.A. Mermaids, an artistic swimming team, but you might know the sport as synchronized swimming. If you've ever wanted to learn how to dance in the water, we will be holding our first general meeting next week. You don't need experience. You just need to have basic swimming skills. There will be flyers up on the bulletin board with a number to call if you have any questions. I hope to see you there."

Synchronized swimming team. How cool is that?

"That was amazing," I say.

"Yeah," Joanne says. "It probably costs lots of money."

Maybe it does. Maybe it doesn't. I'm here to be the center of attention. To be strong and beautiful and graceful. To be lifted up to the sky. You probably have to be so fit to do the things they did. Imagine dancing in the water.

Before I head home, I make sure to grab a flyer.

CHAPTER 2

The only good thing about growing up with a bunch of boys is I get my own room. My sanctuary. The sign attached to the door actually reads NAT'S DOMAIN. No one is allowed in unless they knock—even Dad respects my space. He always uses a special knock. He bangs to the rhythm of an old hip-hop song called "La Di Da Di," like he's doing right now. His tapping allows me more than enough time to hide the new *Vogue* issue. God, I love the looks this month. I tuck the magazine into my hiding place between the mattress and the box spring.

"Enter," I say.

"Reina, breakfast is about to be served." Dad always calls the women in our house *queens*. He's really into compliments and positive reinforcement. He wears an East Los Angeles College T-shirt. He owns way too many of them. My guess is they've given him one every year he's taught there.

I sit at the dining room table while Dad serves me French toast with a huge glob of melting butter in the center. Saturday is the only day Mom sleeps in, which means Dad is in the kitchen doing what he loves to do: cooking. Breakfast is his specialty, so weekends are the days he goes all out. How lucky am I to wake up to bacon sizzling and extra-syrupy French toast?

Ramón saunters in with his usual explosion of curly hair. When we walked back from the pool yesterday, I wouldn't let up about his friend Beto owing me money, to the point where Ramón handed me five dollars to shut up. I reminded him the bet was for ten, but at least I got paid something.

"Good morning," he mumbles, and joins me at the table.

I live for mornings like this one. I love knowing Mom is sleeping in her bedroom, not stressing about the next important meeting she has to attend or the pile of work she has to tackle. I like how Ramón has a sleepy face and electric hair. And I like how happy Dad gets eating his French toast.

Joanne's family is not like this. Her father has been in and out of their lives ever since she was a baby. Her mother works at a factory in Vernon. There's never enough money. That's why I always bring a little extra with me whenever we meet at the pool, just in case Joanne wants to eat a bag of potato chips.

It's not like my family is rolling in dough. We're not, although my parents make sure we get to do the things we like.

"Joy is revolutionary." Another one of Mom's favorite lines.

While we talk about our plans for the rest of the day, we hear the bathroom door shut. Dad heads to the kitchen and soon returns with glasses of orange juice for Ramón and me and a large mug of black coffee for Mom.

Mom.

She's wearing an ELAC T-shirt, too. It's so oversized, it's a minidress on her. Even though she just woke up, she radiates. Her long wavy hair is up in a messy bun. Her glasses are nestled atop her head. Her complexion is only slightly sun-kissed. I think my favorite Mom is this Mom. The one in a tee and not in a suit. The one who doesn't have her cell phone stuck to her hand. The one who isn't in front of a microphone about to give an angry speech.

Mom ruffles my hair and gives Ramón a kiss on the forehead.

"Good morning, my loves," she says. "I feel like I haven't seen you both in forever."

Mom works as an administrator at ELAC. She's also involved in what seems to be a part of every single community-run organization. There's always a meeting or an action. A local newspaper ran a feature on her. They called her the Energizer Bunny of East L.A. Mom complained to the newspaper about them equating her to a bunny, but I think she secretly liked it.

"Mom, I beat Beto in a race yesterday. The full length of the pool," I say. "It was easy."

"She also tried to extort money from him," Ramón says.

Dad hands Mom a plate of scrambled egg whites with a slice of avocado. She gives me a disapproving look, the one I always seem to get. "Nat, we talked about this. No gambling."

"I'm not gambling. I'm betting them that I can beat—"

"Same difference," Ramón interrupts.

"No, it's not."

Why is Ramón defending his dumb friend instead of praising me for outswimming him? Why does he always do that?

"Enough, please," Mom says. "First, I'm glad you were able to teach Beto a lesson on gender roles. However, there is no need for you to do so for money."

"Yes, there is," I mumble.

"Excuse me?" she says.

"Mom. I consider his payment to be a contribution to my, um, like a scholarship to those who can't afford to attend cons."

I'm almost certain she loves my answer, because she's trying really hard to hide her smile behind the coffee mug. Ramón shakes his head.

"No more gambling."

"Yes, Mom," I reluctantly say. I wish she would understand my point of view. It's not gambling. I'm getting paid for educating Beto. It's services rendered.

"Besides that, what is going on?" Mom says. "Ramón?"

Ramón is spending this summer taking an online course on creating video games. Plus, he's in a band (he plays keyboard). Ramón is similar to Mom in that they are always working on five hundred things at once.

"Is it okay if Sheila takes Nat to the pool and back?" Ramón asks. "I was hoping to catch up on some of my work from the course."

"Hmm, I don't know how I feel about that," says Mom. "We agreed you would earn money this summer by being in charge of Nat. Laying the burden on Sheila just because she's family is not fair or what we discussed."

Mom has her business voice on. She does this even with me. I think she doesn't feel Sheila is a good influence on me. I like Sheila, though. I can talk to her about makeup, which is especially important when I'm not even allowed to wear lip gloss.

"It's not for the whole summer—just when I'm behind," Ramón says. "I will pay Sheila out of the money I get from you."

Dad joins us at the table. "I'm okay with it."

"Do I get a say in this?" I say, and Dad and Mom look over to me. Sometimes I feel as if I'm a small bullet point in their large schedule of life. Ramón hates me because he's the last of the boys and stuck with me. I just want to be free to do whatever I want—earn money, look at my magazines, and talk to Joanne. And try to avoid getting into trouble. "Why can't I go to the pool by myself? I know where it is. Joanne and I can walk there together."

Mom and Dad smile.

"Nice try," Dad says. "You're too young."

A ding goes off on Mom's phone. That's it for our family reunion. She has to get ready for a meeting about an upcoming rally. She gulps down her coffee and gives Dad a long kiss. Ramón makes a gross vomiting noise. I don't. My parents are in love. I think it's nice. After they kiss, I follow Mom to her bedroom.

"You okay, fierce one?" she asks as I plop myself on her bed.

Mom and I have very different shapes. She's thin, while I'm a gorda. There are times when I feel people judge us, as if they think I should be as thin as Mom, as if my weight is some sort of failure on her part.

One time at a community action to save a park, I went up to the food vendor to order a second helping of tacos. They were delicious, and I wanted more. I had my money. The lady, for whatever reason, said this to me: "No tacos for your mom? You don't have a problem eating. Ah! You're eating more than enough for both of you." Then she patted her belly while looking at my stomach.

She was joking, I guess. I'm fat and proud, but something about the way she talked to me made me doubt things. I was in such a good mood until her words started to poke at me. I sat down next to my mom and just stared at my plate. I didn't feel like eating anymore. Mom knew something was wrong right away, but I didn't want to tell on the lady. Why was I protecting her? I guess maybe I thought she was right, that I was eating too much.

"Fierce one, what's wrong? Did something happen?" Mom asked.

"No, just that . . . the taquera said something, you know, about me eating for both of us. She was trying to be funny," I said, feeling shy and uncomfortable. "It's okay. I'm not really hungry."

"Oh? Come with me." Mom took my hand and walked right up to the woman. "Don't ever make my daughter or anyone else feel bad in regards to their eating. She's her own person and she doesn't have to look like me or anyone else."

The taquera was insulted at first. "No pasa nada," she said, not really looking at us. Mom stayed calm. She didn't raise her voice once. Plus, she did it all in Spanish. "My daughter is beautiful," Mom said. The taquera nodded. "Now, please apologize to her." The woman was slightly annoyed, but she did say sorry. Mom is pretty badass.

"What do you think about synchronized swimming?" I ask now, from her bed.

Mom barely looks up from her phone.

"Do you mean synchronized swimming, like Esther Williams?"

"Esther Williams? Who is that? No, I mean like dancing in the water. Girls doing the same thing at the same time."

She takes a sip from her favorite mug. The mug reads GREATEST CHINGONA OF ALL TIME.

"In the fifties, Esther Williams popularized synchronized swimming in the movies," she says. "It's very beautiful and glossy, but I think the sport overlooks strength for stylized costumes and streamlined bodies. Go look at some videos and you'll see what I mean."

Mom always talks to me like an adult. Class. Body positivity. These are important topics in this house. What she doesn't know is that I spent last night looking up synchronized swimming videos, and I couldn't stop playing them over and over. The sequins. The wild makeup. The expressions. It was awesome. I guess I should have known Mom would think there was something demeaning about dancing in the water in public. I still like it, though. Does it make me less of a feminist if I like something so pretty?

Mom continues to get ready for her meeting.

"Anything else you want to tell me?" she asks.

"Nope. Just that it was fun beating Beto, that's all."

She laughs, shaking her head a bit.

"My rebel," she says, hugging me. "Have a good day. Make good choices."

I head back to my room.

Now to find out who Esther Williams is.

CHAPTER 3

I'm on my third viewing of the old movie *Million Dollar Mermaid*. Now I understand what people mean when they say a movie was made in Technicolor. The colors are so intense, it's as if the movie people decided to use a special filter to make them super vivid. As for the costumes, I've never seen anything like them. It's all so extra. *Extra* extra. I love it.

Esther Williams is the star, and she's wow. It's exactly like what those synchronized swimmers did in the pool the other day, but way more intricate. The swimmers look like a gang, a gang of girls ready to out-flip whoever dares approach them. Imagine being in the middle of those girls. Me, in the center of a circle of swimmers.

I stand in front of my full-length mirror. It's been a while, but I think I can still do a split. I do a couple of quick stretches and then start to slowly lower my body.

When I was in third grade, I bet this girl Rosa her school snacks for a week if I could do a complete split. She said my stomach was too big, there was no way I could be so flexible. She said girls like me couldn't even touch their toes. I didn't even hesitate. I dropped right down on the cafeteria floor. For a whole week, Rosa forked over a bag of chocolate chip cookies every day, just for me.

"What are you doing?" Ramón asks. He entered my room without knocking, which is a huge violation.

"Get out!"

"Sorry. We need to go. Please, Nat, for once, will you work with me?"

Because he apologizes, I let the trespassing infraction pass. I dust myself off and gather my things. I really need to work on my split. I'm too rusty. Ramón waits by the door.

"What's the big rush?" I ask.

"Band practice and homework. Sheila is going to look after you."

My brother's band is called the Boyle Heights Brothers. I've heard them play before. They aren't very good. I think they're going for an old-school vibe like Chicano Batman minus the matching suits. Dad thinks they have talent. Then again, Dad wants Ramón to live out his own rock-and-roll dreams.

"Hey, did you know Esther Williams was from Inglewood?"

Ramón has extra-long legs. It's hard to catch up to him while he walks. We first have to head over to Sheila's house. We'll pick up Joanne on the way to the pool.

"Who?"

"Esther Williams, the synchronized swimmer. She was big in the fifties." I pull up an image I saved on my phone. Ramón takes a quick look.

"She's pretty," he says. "Why Esther Williams?"

The cool thing about Ramón is even when he's slightly annoyed about being stuck with me, he doesn't always treat me like the plague. Sure, he didn't stick up for me with Beto, but that's not always the case. There was that time I almost came to blows with my next-door neighbor. The boy insisted on calling me Natalia instead of Nat, even after I corrected him multiple times. I guess one day I wasn't having it and I lost my cool, but before I did something I would really regret, Ramón took the boy aside and explained the importance of names and naming. The boy shrugged and apologized. Ramón is pretty calm, like my dad. I could use some of that. I need to learn how to be a bit more diplomatic.

"No reason. I just think it's cool. Kicks and jumps in the water," I say. "Mom thinks it's too belittling to women. Synchronized swimming, that is."

Ramón chuckles.

"Yeah, well, Mom thinks everything is questionable. Remember when she wouldn't let me take you to watch the movie *Coco* because she thought the afterlife shouldn't have any borders or border patrol?"

It took a while for Mom to give in, but eventually she let

us watch *Coco*. I liked the film, but it's hard to completely fall in love with something when someone points out a wrong in it.

I keep sharing Esther Williams trivia and Ramón doesn't seem to mind.

Sheila wears the reddest lipstick ever. It makes her lips look like stop signs. Her tank top is blue and her cutoff jeans barely cover her nalgas. I'm kind of in awe. Ramón's friends always follow Sheila around like puppies.

"What's the name of your lipstick?" I ask her.

"It's called Stunna."

Stunna. Imagine having a job where you come up with names for lipsticks. I would be so good at that.

Ramón hands money to Sheila, and we head on our way to pick Joanne up. Adventures at the pool. I only hope there are new victims I can take on. There's money to be made today. I feel lucky. I can feel it in the air.

"Ever heard of Esther Williams?"

Sheila shakes her head. "No, who is Esther Williams?"

I go on about Esther Williams and how she couldn't make it to the Olympics. Instead, she ended up training alongside the guy who played Tarzan on television. Someone noticed her swimming skills, and she joined the Aquacade, a synchronized swimming team.

"Then a movie guy discovered her and put her in films. Pretty cool, huh?"

Sheila eyes the picture on my phone. I can tell she likes

it just like me. Sheila and I are alike. I need someone on my side who loves fashion and beauty as much as I do. She knows about my stash of magazines. To avoid getting busted by Mom, I hand them over to her when I'm done. Sheila's mom is not like my mom. She allows Sheila to wear pretty much whatever she wants. Sheila has kissed boys before. She's cool.

"For today, do not get into any fights," Sheila says.

"I can't promise anything."

She shakes her head. "There's going to be a time when you will no longer feel the need to fight."

I can't stop laughing. Mom says we are in a constant struggle, and I'm born to be a warrior. A WARRIOR. Also, I don't view my confrontations as fights. I view them as misunderstandings and teachable moments.

"You ever been in a fight?"

Sheila flips her hair. She spends a lot of time making sure her hair is blow-dried straight. It would be a dream to be able to commit to beauty every morning like her, but Mom would never allow it. If Mom would let me, I would spend so many hours figuring out what to wear and doing my makeup. If only.

"Yeah," she says. "Her name was Brenda. She kept talking about me at school, so I had to put her in her place."

See. Even Sheila can't deny that teachable moments have to be forced.

"I ended up suspended from school *and* punished at home."

"*But* it was worth it," I say.

"No, it wasn't it. Brenda still talks about me behind my back. It didn't stop her. Haters will continue to hate," Sheila says. "If they're talking about you, it only means they're jealous. Don't forget it."

I guess she's right. Sometimes I don't like it when kids call me names. The only thing that stops their dumb mouths from going on is a fist. My skin isn't thick enough. Words hurt.

"Hi, Nat!" Joanne says.

Only Joanne would bring a heavy bag filled with books to the pool. She's gearing up for the con, reading up on everything, including everyone who will be attending. She also studies which booths will be giving out freebies so we can scope them out first. Today we're deciding which panels will be worth attending. The conference is not until October, four months from now, but it never hurts to be prepared. Besides, I have to figure out what I'm going to wear. The costumes take time to create.

"I feel lucky today," I whisper to her. Joanne never joins me in my bets. She's way too shy for any of my business propositions. She's good for advice, though, and I go to her for everything.

"I have to tell you something," Joanne says. This doesn't sound good. I feel my nerves tighten.

"What's going on?"

"Mom was let go from her job."

Man. The worst news ever. Joanne doesn't cry, but it looks like she's about to. I place my arm around her shoulders. Her bag is so heavy. I take it from her and carry it.

"I'm so sorry. What is she going to do?"

"Look for another. Dad left early this morning, but I heard them arguing. They want me to try to find a way to make money."

Make money? How can Joanne get a job? There are laws against kids our age working.

"How?"

"I have an aunt who just had a baby. I'll probably have to help her with him."

"But what about our summer? The pool? The con?"

Joanne wrings her hands. I know enough to stop talking, because although this is the way I deal with things—I think things out loud—this only makes her feel worse.

"Hey! I have more than enough saved to take care of us at the con and whatever else we'll need," I say. "Things will work out."

Joanne nods. Money woes are a lot for anyone to deal with. I wish someone could sponsor her life. I make a note in my head to ask Mom about possible jobs. Mom is a great connector of people. I'm sure she will know someone. I don't want to spend this summer without Joanne by my side.

We arrive at the pool and she drops the subject.

Inside, Sheila places her towel in a shady part. The pool is its own world. The abuelas are ready to take a water aerobics class with Flavio. I notice Beto chatting up some girl. I give him the stink eye.

That's when I spot her. My next victim. The girl is probably a couple of years older than me. She's white, so she sticks out more than most people. It's okay. I don't discriminate when it comes to making money. When she enters the pool, she casually swims across. Her strokes are a little on the lazy side.

I swim over to her and give her a nod.

"Hi," I say. "You want to race?"

I ask her this quietly. There's no need to alert the masses. Sometimes business interactions can be done on the hush.

"Sure."

We do a lap and I let her get ahead of me. I want her to believe she's a better swimmer. We race again and she beats me by only a few seconds. The third time is when I lay out the rules.

"I think I can beat you. Want to bet?"

The girl eyes me with apprehension.

"Ten bucks. Swim the full length of the pool. Want in?"

A few minutes later, she hands me the crumpled ten

dollars. She's not like Beto, who is a sore loser and will never amount to much of anything because of his weak self. Or at least it's what I want to imagine. I hand the money over to Joanne, who places it in her bag. I scan the pool for another person to race.

"Who's that talking to Sheila?" asks Joanne.

Sheila is arguing with a boy. Oh no. I don't like the way he keeps pointing his finger at her face. Joanne and I walk over.

"Why you being such a b——?"

That's it. The one word I cannot stand. I don't care how big he is, how old he is, or whatever. He doesn't get to call my cousin the B word. Before Joanne can even try to stop me, I'm in the guy's face.

"How dare you!"

Maybe I'm in my feelings about Joanne. Maybe I don't like the way this boy keeps calling my cousin disgusting words. I don't know what comes over me, but all I see is red. I jump him and start pounding. The boy is on the floor. He tries to protect his face, but I'm using him like a punching bag. I'm giving him everything I got.

Someone drags me away. There's a crowd now. When I look over at Sheila, I expect her to be happy. I'm defending her. But no. The look she has is far from happiness. She's pissed because I did the one thing I wasn't supposed to do: I got into a fight.

CHAPTER 4

Roosevelt Pool is off-limits to me for a whole week, maybe even two. Christian, the pool manager, actually wants to kick me out for good. Sheila tries to convince him otherwise.

"There's no fighting here. You know better than that," Christian says. We're in the pool office. "How long you've been coming here? Since you were barely walking. Your parents used to hang out here. Your grandparents. How do you think they would feel knowing you out here fighting people?"

My grandmother's nickname was Shorty. They called her Shorty not because she was short, although she was. They called her Shorty because she had a short fuse, as in she would blow up really quickly. Her real name was Natalia. I'm named after her. Although I was very young when she passed away, I'm almost a hundred percent sure she would have done the same thing.

"What about him?" I point to the boy who is getting a

talking-to at the far end of the room. "What happens to him?"

"See? This is the problem," Christian says. "You shouldn't worry about what happens to other people. Keep your side of the street clean."

I like Christian because there were times when he let me come into the pool right before it opened. Joanne and I had full access to the whole place. Of course, right now I can't stand his guts because he is not listening to me. The boy was disrespecting my cousin. I had to do something. Didn't I?

"What am I supposed to do with her for a whole week?" Sheila says. "This is our only outlet."

Christian is not budging. Not one bit. This isn't the first time he's had to call me in to his office. I don't understand why today is different. Usually, he would just give me a good talking-to and send me home to return the next day.

Maybe if I started to cry. If only I could be like those telenovela actresses who can squeeze out tears at the drop of a hat. I try to think of all kinds of sad things, but nothing works. It's probably because I still want to punch him.

Outside, Joanne presses her face against the window. She uses her book to cover her head from the glare of the sun.

"Why do you have to make things so difficult? The guy is an idiot. I was handling the situation," Sheila yells. "I didn't ask you to come over and hit him in the head. Did I?"

No, she didn't ask, but I've been taught that every single person must defend those who are defenseless. Also, family before anything. However, I know well enough to keep quiet when Sheila gets like this. Anything I say or do will only anger her more.

Sheila pleads with Christian to let us back in. They take their conversation over to the side, away from me.

The boy who called Sheila the B word is about to leave. Sheila and Christian are too busy with their talk. I look over at Joanne. She can tell what I'm thinking, and she vigorously shakes her head.

I don't care. I walk over to the guy anyway.

"You better stay away from us. The next time I won't be so kind."

He doesn't say anything.

"Nat!"

Oops.

"Get over here!" There is nothing Stunna about Sheila's expression right now. I grab my bag and follow her as she storms out. Joanne trails slightly behind.

"Why? Nat, why?" Sheila says. Her arms flail about as if she's delivering an important speech. "I asked you not to fight, and what do you do? What am I going to say to Aunt Angela?"

The solution is simple to me: Don't tell Mom. She

doesn't have to know what's going on. Not at all.

Sheila stops in front of the Artic Hotspot Café, then goes in. Joanne and I wait outside.

"She's really mad," Joanne says.

"Yeah."

"Have you been trying the meditation app?"

The last time I got into a fight, Joanne took it upon herself to send me a bunch of links to articles on how to manage your anger. The meditation app was one of the suggestions. I tried it. The woman's voice was way too suspicious-sounding. I kept thinking how I didn't trust her. Now, if the app came in my mother's voice or some-one who sounds like me, then maybe.

"I think my situation is beyond the help of an app." I'm starting to feel the weight of my actions. I wish I could be like Joanne. Why can't her quietness rub off on me? Why do I always do things without thinking them through first?

"What should I do?"

"Well," Joanne says. "You have to say sorry. First, make sure you understand why you're apologizing. Sheila can tell when you're lying."

Joanne is right. Sheila can smell when I'm putting on an act.

"C'mon." Sheila exits the store and heads to the park. The heat is really soaring now, and I wished more than anything that I was in the cold, chlorinated water.

Sheila plops down on a bench and angrily sips her juice. We sit in silence. In the quiet, I can see where I went wrong. They are right. I shouldn't have reacted the way I did. I'm always flying off the handle. Dad says it's because I haven't learned how to filter myself. He thinks that will come with experience and age. I'm almost twelve. If I'm not filtering myself now, when will I?

Joanne nudges me.

"Sorry, Sheila." I mean it, too. My anger always finds a way of getting me in the worst trouble. "I didn't mean for us to get kicked out of the pool. I should have minded my own business. The guy wasn't talking to me. I need to keep my side clean, like Christian says."

Sheila was basically the first girl in our family. She once told me Mom used to baby her like she was her own daughter. When I came along, Sheila did the same to me. I was her doll until Mom didn't appreciate the overly feminine dresses Sheila insisted I wear.

She lets out a long sigh.

"That idiot's been asking me out for days. When I finally told him I wasn't interested, he played himself. Men can be so predictable," she says. "I'm glad you hit him, just not glad you got busted for it."

"Do you have to tell my parents?"

Sheila pulls out her mirror and reapplies her lipstick. I can't wait until I'm able to do the same.

"What am I going to do with you?" she says. Sheila

won't rat me out. A true cousin through and through. "You're too much."

"Maybe if you did some chants, we wouldn't be in this predicament," Joanne says.

Joanne shows Sheila the meditation app. Sheila can't stop laughing. She taps the app and places an earbud in her ear. The other one she gives to me. I listen to the voice. It's so hard. I just want to run up and down the park. I want to scare the squirrels. I want to go down the slide.

"Close your eyes, Nat."

"What if someone walks behind us and tries to scare us?"

"Close. Your. Eyes."

I finally shut them and try my best to concentrate on what the suspicious voice says. It's hard to quell the noise in my head, but I give it a chance. Really listen to the words: "As you breathe, just feel your body soften. Notice the feeling of your body, your weight pressing down on the seat. Notice the sounds around you. . . ." We stay like this for what feels like an eternity. How are people meant to stay calm? If anything, I feel extremely nervous and wired. When the session is done, do I feel changed? Not really. I guess I should try to do it every day. I don't know.

"Now what?" I ask. It's still too early to go home. Sweat is pooling on my neck. I don't want to go home, and I can tell Sheila doesn't want to go, either.

"Screw it," she says. "Let's go."

"Where?" Both Joanne and I say at the same time.

"Ouch!" I scream when Joanne punches me on the arm to break the jinx. "So where we going?"

"Don't worry about it," Sheila says. "Follow me."

Before we know it, we're boarding the bus heading to Exposition Park. We're taking a total detour, and I don't know what to expect. Joanne and I giggle as we follow Sheila.

When we arrive, we press our faces to the gate. Although I've been to the nearby Natural History Museum, I've never been to the Exposition Park pool. The place is way bigger than Roosevelt. There is an Olympic-size pool with a splash pad for kids and so much room.

We join a line of people waiting to pay admission to get in.

"This is going to be good," I say. Joanne agrees.

Sheila pays the entrance fee and we enter. We walk over to the front desk to ask for information from the pool clerk, who has super-short hair and a nice smile.

"Are you sisters?" the pool clerk asks.

"No. Cousins and friends," Sheila responds. "It's on me to take care of them."

"Cool. Well, there's always something happening here. You won't be bored," she says. "My name is Kim. Let me know if you need anything."

Joanne and I spend hours in the splash pad. I think we

are totally regressing—to the point the little kids give us side-eye.

"Do you think Sheila will bring us here for the rest of the week? Roosevelt doesn't compare at all," Joanne says.

"Who knows? Maybe she wanted a change," I say. "I'm fine with that. Okay, I got to pee."

We walk back inside and use the restrooms.

"Are you hungry?" I say. "I'll be right back."

While Joanne is in the bathroom, I explore. There are a bunch of pictures taken from when the Olympics were held here. Swimmers in their retro bathing suits. It's just like in those Esther Williams films. I wonder if she ever took a dip here. I can imagine the crowds of people cheering on the swimmers.

I find the vending machines and buy a couple of chocolate bars. One for Joanne. One for me. I walk over to the bulletin board and spy a familiar bright orange flyer.

The L.A. Mermaids practice here. How freaking cool! Today didn't turn out to be totally crap. The flyer also states the time of their next meeting. ALL ARE WELCOME is written in bold letters.

"You need to be in good shape to be able to do that." The man's voice comes out of nowhere. I try to ignore him, but he won't stop talking.

"It's a whole-body sport," he continues. "You must be able to swim and dance and be strong."

I turn to him. The man gives me the up and down, but the funny thing is, both of our bellies stick out. Maybe he thinks just because I'm fat, I can't do it.

"Are you in charge of the team or something?" I ask.

The man shakes his head. "I've been going to this pool for longer than you've been breathing," he says. "If you're even considering joining the team, you gotta stop eating those."

He points to my chocolate bar. So rude. Out of spite, I take a big bite and snatch the flyer from the bulletin board. Then I stomp over to the front desk.

"Can I go to this meeting?"

Kim reads the flyer and nods.

"Of course you can. It's tomorrow, upstairs in conference room B," she says, and then leans in. "And don't listen to him. All he does is swim one lap a day and spend the rest of his day giving advice no one asked for. He swears he's a better swimmer than Michael Phelps."

Jerk. At least I didn't do what I normally would: throw the chocolate bar in his face. The meditation app must be working.

I go looking for Joanne and show her the flyer.

"Look at this!"

She reads it. "What does this have to do with me?"

I point to the guy who's about to do his one lap.

"He thinks I'm too fat to join the synchronized swimming team," I say.

"What do you care what he says?" Sheila says.

Sheila and Joanne don't get it. Although I've never met this random person before, he's issued me a challenge. He doesn't know this, but he did. He thinks I can't do it. I am here to prove to him and every other guy that I can.

"You're not going to join the team, are you?" Joanne asks.

Joanne's giving me a worried look mixed with a little excitement. Out of everyone in the whole wide world, she knows all too well that something is about to happen. She can feel it. So can I.

"Why?" I ask. "You don't think I can do it?"

"I know you can do it," Joanne says. "That's the problem."

"The meeting is tomorrow. We are coming back, right, Sheila?"

Sheila presses her Stunna lips together. Kim from the front desk walks past us and gives us a nod. Sheila smiles at her.

"Maybe."

Her maybe is a definite yes. We'll be back. And tomorrow, I will check out the L.A. Mermaids.

The guy does his one lap and starts to guzzle down a Gatorade bottle as if he completed a swim competition.

Just you wait, Mr. So-Not-Michael-Phelps.

CHAPTER 5

Last night I dreamt I was wearing an Esther Williams getup, the one in the final swim sequence of the mermaid movie. In the dream, Esther Williams decided to hand over the spotlight to an unknown swimmer, a brown girl who never stepped foot into a pool before but for some reason was a total natural. I, of course, was the brown girl. Everyone told her she was making a mistake. No one wanted to see this fat girl in the water. The other swimmers were complaining about having to lift me. It didn't matter. Esther Williams was adamant. I was going to be the one.

On the verge of tears, I decided to go on with the show. Before I did, I gave this amazing speech about loving your body. The haters started to cry from emotions. Then we did our perfect water dance and they lifted me up in the air. I was a total perfect ten.

Unfortunately, I awake not in an Esther Williams sequined outfit, but in my messy room.

The meeting for the L.A. Mermaids is today. Restless

butterflies invade my stomach. It's the same feeling I get before the first day of school, but way more intense. I get up from under my pile of clothes and start to get ready.

"Did you get kicked out of the pool yesterday?"

Ramón corners me on my way to the bathroom.

"Not necessarily." I need Ramón to keep this conversation on a whole other level of quiet.

"Beto said you were fighting a guy and Christian blacklisted you."

"His facts are wrong. It's not what happened."

Ramón pulls me into his room. Unlike my room, where it's an explosion of crap everywhere, Ramón's room is immaculate. Nothing is out of place. I sit down on his desk chair.

He turns the chair to face him. "Spill it."

"C'mon, Ramón, this is silly."

He crosses his arms and glares. He's not fooling around. I have no choice but to tell the truth.

"I got into a fight and Christian kicked me out for a week," I say. "The cool thing is I downloaded this great meditation app, which I will be using every day from now on. I swear. Problem solved."

Ramón and I like to attend MMA fights. In fact, we have tickets to a bout in a couple of weeks. Dad likes the fights, too, but not Mom, who only approves "fighting the man." So maybe there have been times when Ramón has taught me some wrestling maneuvers. Maybe we've looked up

YouTube MMA moves and practiced. Technically, my fighting stems from these things. Don't they? Isn't he a bit to blame for my maladjusted ways?

"Don't worry. Sheila took us to the Exposition Park pool," I say. "It's all good."

"This wasn't what we agreed on. If Mom finds out about Roosevelt, we're both going to get in trouble."

I don't see how my getting blacklisted from the pool affects his world. Sheila is still taking care of me. I haven't even had a chance to tell him about the synchronized swimming team yet. Ramón stresses out too much. Everything will work out. My dream was a definite sign.

"It's only for a week. Please don't tell her."

Ramón grabs my shoulders.

"Will you take a breather before reacting? Pause."

"Pause," I say. "I promise."

Before I came along, Ramón was the baby of the house. He said when I first arrived from the hospital, the first thing he asked Mom was if they could exchange me for a boy. I think he's held on to that resentment.

"I'm going to be playing my first gig," Ramón says while he gathers his stuff. "Gotta practice every chance I get. With work and summer school, there isn't much time."

"Are you getting paid?"

"Exposure."

Exposure? Who does anything for exposure? Ramón needs a manager, someone who can look out for him.

"I can help you get exposure."

"No!" he cuts me off before I continue. "Nat, I know you mean well, but why don't we stick to the things we need to do this summer—you staying out of trouble, and me finishing this summer course. Deal?"

"Sure, big brother."

I decide not to tell Ramón about the meeting. There's no point. He asked me to pause, and in doing so I didn't find any valuable reason to tell him. Besides, I probably won't be able to join the team, so there's no point.

Today Sheila's lipstick color is called Ya Dig. It's this intense blue. Instead of letting her long hair down, she has it in two French braids. To match her lips, she wears her cutoff jeans and a blue tank top.

"Where's your sidekick?" she asks.

Joanne's babysitting gig starts today and there's nothing I can do about it. I told her I needed her for the meeting, but she couldn't come.

"Joanne is not my sidekick. We're equals," I say.

"Okay, what's going on? Are you upset or something?"

My tone is off. I guess I'm angry. I wish Joanne was here and not babysitting. I wish money wasn't ever an issue in her life. I wish I won the lottery.

"Sorry. I must be nervous."

"Nervous, you? I can't believe what I'm hearing. This is the same girl who outswims everyone, young or old. The same girl who not two days ago defended me from some loser. Just jumped right in," she says. "You're pretty fear-less. Just remember, try not to punch anyone."

I don't necessarily feel fearless. Although my mother is all about empowering me, I'm still filled with doubt. Mom tells me to use my rage to get what I want. It doesn't work all the time.

A couple of years ago, there was an incident at school. A group of kids decided my name was going to be Fat instead of Nat. Pretty clever, huh? I tried my best to ignore them. It was tiring to hear them call me that, even in whispers. So instead of wearing my normal uniform of the tightest clothes, I started to wear oversized shirts. It was a dead giveaway that something was wrong.

At dinner, Mom, Dad, and Ramón asked me what was up. I tried to keep it to myself. I even got mad at them. I told them not everything can be fixed with a fight. Sometimes I just want to be left alone.

"Never allow others to silence your beauty and your strength," Mom said. "They don't get to win. We do."

Soon after, the school was notified. Parents called in. It was kind of a big deal. Still, in a tiny spot hidden way inside of me, I feel maybe I shouldn't always be so in your face. I don't know. With Ramón telling me to pause, Sheila telling me to stop, and Joanne with her meditation app, signs are pointing me to practice taking way less space.

"Sheila, what if they say I can't join because of . . . you know?"

Sheila stops walking. She turns to me and I can see a little of how we are related. I mean, she's light-skinned, not dark like me, but we have the same eyes and nose.

"Do you want some lipstick?"

I feel like bursting out of my body. Yes, I want to feel Ya Dig. Have my lips painted blue like a science-fiction road warrior.

"I'm only going to put a little bit. Just enough to be noticeable, okay?"

When she's done, I stare at my reflection using my phone. *Fearless* is the word that comes to mind.

The conference room is located upstairs on the second floor. Joanne said I should walk in with a pen and a notebook so I look professional. The only notebook I could find has a picture of Justin Bieber on the cover. I have inked an anime hairdo on him because no one should judge me for being a Belieber way back when.

Outside of the conference room are a bunch of girls. The L.A. Mermaids. A few of them are braiding each other's hair. Others are listening to music on their phones. One of them nods a hello to me. I nod back.

"Okay, Joanne, I'm going in. Wish me luck," I text.

Joanne sends me a whole bunch of emojis before I turn on the Do Not Disturb on the phone.

I peek inside the room. There are barely any chairs left. Mothers, some with their younger kids, occupy most of the seats. I hold tight to my notebook and walk in.

"There are seats in the back." A young woman motions to an empty seat. Before I go, she also hands me a stack of papers. Schedules, rules, the history of the team. Another woman moves her handbag from a chair, and I sit down.

"As I said, welcome to all the potential new L.A. Mermaids and returning families. My name is Renée Williams, and I'm the founder and owner of the L.A. Mermaids artistic swimming team," she says.

Renée is Black, tall, and wears a bright orange T-shirt with L.A. MERMAIDS on it. Her arms are muscular like an MMA fighter's, and I wish mine looked just like that. But I'm confused.

"I thought it was called synchronized swimming?" I call out. "Am I in the wrong room?"

Renée chuckles. "No, you're not. In 2017, the Swimming Federation changed the name, but between us, I sometimes call it synchronized swimming. Okay, let's move forward. There's a lot to cover."

Thank goodness. For a second there, I thought I was in an art class. Moments later, a tall, lanky boy walks into the room and sits beside me. He looks about my age.

"I like the blond tips in your hair," I say. I do. It's pretty cool. I went through a period of wanting to dye my hair purple or blue, but natural is always best, Mom says.

"Thanks."

His mother, or who I think is his mother, shushes him.

"Last year was one of our strongest competitive years. This year, we will be including trips to San Diego, Arizona, and of course, the goal is to make it to the Junior Olympics. And we'll do it! I feel really good about it."

A young woman beside her translates what Renée says into Spanish. Renée explains how she started synchronized swimming when she was seven years old. Seven years old! I wonder if she had a pool in her house. How else would she have been able to practice?

While Renée prepares to go over another topic on her agenda, I look around. The adults are from all backgrounds. Latines. Blacks. Asians. It's a real mix.

The boy next to me doodles a tiny sketch of the coach right beside his notes. The drawing is pretty good. His notes are so neat, too. I should probably take notes.

"Are you joining the team?" I whisper.

"Maybe," he says. "My name is Daniel."

"Hi, I'm Nat. Nice to meet you."

His mother also shakes my hand and introduces herself. She's way younger than Mom.

"Is your mother here?" she asks.

"No, she couldn't make it. She's busy."

The mother nods in understanding.

There's a handout for each topic Renée talks about. I try my best to keep up. Swimmers must be between the ages of seven to nineteen. There will be a Saturday dedicated to testing the levels of swimmers. I wonder what level I would be. I'm fast, but I don't think I can do those underwater flips or ballet legs or whatever other stuff Renée talks about. Sometimes she uses terms I've never heard about, but others in the room seem to get it. Synchronized swimming is a whole new world and one with its own language.

Then Renée comes to the part I was waiting for—money talk.

"Once you pass the assessment, we'll have another meeting to go over monthly dues and fees. I hope to see you this weekend."

What? I was really hoping she would cover numbers. I can't really make a commitment if I don't know how much it's going to cost. After about an hour and a half, the meeting ends. Renée is surrounded by people asking her questions. I need to get my question in there, too. I shove to the front of the crowd. A couple of the adults look annoyed, but who cares. I need to know about the money.

"Excuse me. Excuse me, miss."

Renée finally notices me.

"Hi. I saw you walk in," she says. "What's your name?"

I tell her my name and she asks if I'll be at the tryouts.

"Maybe, but first, how much is this going to cost?"

Renée laughs. "Tryouts are free. The other costs we will have to go over once you get on the team."

I don't know. I'm not feeling good about this. I like

things to be spelled out, especially when it comes to money.

"Just take a chance," Renée says as if she's reading my mind.

I still need to know if this team is legit.

"Do you know who Esther Williams is?" I ask.

"Of course I know who she is," Renée says with a grin. "But have you ever heard of Anita Alvarez? She competed in the 2016 Olympics, and she's Mexican American."

My eyes practically fall out of my head. A Latina.

Oh, it's so on.

CHAPTER 6

Mom is the problem. The tryouts are today at 2:00 p.m., and Sheila promised to take me. Ramón is doing his thing and Dad is working. It's Mom who's messing up my plans because today, of all days, she wants to spend it with her daughter.

"I have a meeting downtown. Afterward, we can go eat at Guelaguetza," she says. "Sound like a plan?"

She pulls me in for a tight hug and tells me she misses me. Mom's been working long hours and we haven't seen her much. I love Guelaguetza, love the mole with all of my heart, but not today, not when I need to be at Expo. How do I say no to Mom without her becoming suspicious?

"I haven't had a chance to catch up with you. I want to know how your summer is going. Everything."

Mom does this at least once a week. Although she's extremely busy, she always finds time to catch up with us. She probably already has a date set up with Ramón.

"Mom, I have an appointment today."

She looks shocked, especially since I'm actually saying

no to mole. It goes against everything I am.

"Oh," she says. Mom stares at me with her intense hawk eyes, trying to decipher what's going on. "How is it possible your agenda is so jam-packed, you can't spend a little time with your mother?"

Oh boy. Mom is hurt by what I said. She's pouring on the guilt. I have to stay strong.

"Sheila and I have a date," I say.

"Wait a minute. Aren't I paying for Sheila to take care of you? It's not technically a date if it's her job, now, is it?"

Okay, maybe I should have used another excuse.

"I like hanging out with Sheila. Don't you like Sheila?"

"I love Sheila. Why would you say that?"

I pause. How do I say this without sounding too obnoxious? I've heard Mom argue with her sister, my aunt Lupe, about how Sheila spends too much money on makeup. She should be concentrating on school and focusing less on appearances. It's not that Mom doesn't love Sheila—she does. She just wants more from her, like she wants more from everyone, including me.

"You think"—I choose my words carefully—"she's a bad influence on me."

"That's not true."

Uh-oh. Mom is mad.

"It's not true at all. Sheila is a smart girl. With a little nudge in the right direction, she can be and do whatever she wants."

There's a "but" in there somewhere. I can feel it.

"I get upset when I see young girls waste their potential. What is the one thing I always say? 'No one is going to give you a free pass. You have to push and shove your way to the front.'"

I don't see what that has to do with Sheila. So what if she wears makeup and spends a lot of time, I mean a *lot* of time, blowing out her hair. What does that have to do with her potential?

"I like lipstick."

"Lipsticks won't lead a revolution. Will they?"

Why can't a Fenty lipstick lead a revolution? This is how I know Mom would never approve of synchronized swimming. I need to keep my plans a secret.

"We'll reschedule for another day." Mom pulls out her calendar. She has multiple calendars, but the one she swears by is her old-school paper calendar, where she jots everything down, and she carries it with her everywhere she goes.

"Later this week, there's an action being proposed. It's still up in the air. We'll go there," she says. "Sound good?"

An action means we will be marching or protesting. Ever since I can remember, Mom has been really active in the community: Protests. Marches. Board meetings. Community meetings. When you have an active Mom and Dad like I do, you spend a lot of time yelling.

"Sure."

"Hey, I love you in every possible way."

"I love you, too, Mom."

Her phone buzzes, and I know she's off to start her day. I overheard Mom and Dad speak about how she might be running for a seat—school board or community something. They talked about the toll it would place on the family. Her schedule is already so full. Having such a popular Mom is hard. I want her to be everything. I also sometimes just want her to be at home, sort of like Sheila's mom. My aunt Lupe is a stay-at-home mom. She cooks and cleans for her husband, Joe, who works in construction, and for Sheila. She doesn't spend her time at multiple meetings or actions or any of the other things pulling my mom away from me. It's not like Sheila's mom is better than mine. I just wish Mom would sometimes be a little like Aunt Lupe.

And yet I'm the one who told her no. Guilt got me reconsidering my life choices, including not telling Mom about the synchro team tryouts. I wish I could say how I really feel, how I think lipsticks can start revolutions. Makeup can be a type of armor. When I page through the fashion magazines, I'm not stupid. The prices are so out of control, and I know all about who makes the clothes and where. Mom has shown me documentaries. We've protested at factories here in Los Angeles against low living wages and hazardous conditions. The clothes sometimes aren't meant for someone my size. Yet I can see the beauty on those pages. I can enjoy it. If I'm not able to say how I feel, then I'm not being the real me.

Kim is the locker room attendant today, so Sheila hands her our tote bags with our clothes.

"What are you listening to?" Sheila asks. Kim's listening to loud banging rock music off her phone.

"Squid Ink. They're from Fresno. Their lead singer is dope," Kim says. "You like it?"

Sheila nods.

"Sorry, this music is too loud," I say. "Where are the tryouts?"

"Nat!"

"It's okay, it is loud. I like my music loud." Kim laughs. "You, Nat—you belong out in the pool with the rest of the swimmers. Are you trying out, too?" she says to Sheila.

"Me? No," Sheila says. She does the thing where she tosses her hair. "Only my cousin."

"Okay, bye," I say. They continue to talk about local bands and other things I have no time for.

Outside, families sit in the bleachers, getting their kids ready for the tryouts. Other kids listen to their headphones. I notice Daniel, the boy with the frosted tips, and stand beside him.

"Hi," I say.

"Hi," Daniel says. "Are you ready? I heard it's not bad. They want to make sure we can swim and handle directions. My sister used to be a synchronized swim-mer. She told me what to expect."

Even if what he says is true, my butterflies are still wreaking havoc in my belly.

"Everyone here for the tryouts, welcome!" Renée says, approaching with a clipboard. There are a couple of L.A. Mermaids helping her out, older high school girls who are part of the team. "We're going to start now. Please line up."

Daniel and I walk over to the edge of the pool. The team member in charge of our group introduces herself. Her name is Iliana, but she wants us to call her Ili. She has bright blue hair and has been with the team for three years, since she was thirteen, just a year older than me.

"As you can see, there are different stations. At this station, we are going to test your swimming skills. After you're done here, you'll move to the next station to test your treading skills."

"What's treading?" I ask. "What do you mean by sta-tions, and will I be getting a score like in the Olympics?"

Ili tries suppressing a laugh, although I'm sure this is what's on everyone's mind. Also, if I'm going to try out, I want to get a gold medal or at least a gold sticker.

"We are only testing to see what level swimmer you are," she says. "Treading is when you keep your head above the surface of the water, kicking your legs back and forth or in a circle to be able to do that."

Ili groups us together in fives. Daniel is in my group, as are two girls who seem to be friends, and another who definitely doesn't want to be here. Her mother is in the bleachers, yelling out her name. Every time she does, I see the girl recoil inside her oversized towel.

"I really wish she would stop," the girl mutters to herself. I wonder if my mom would ever act that way with me. When I was six, I was in a production of *Peter Pan*. They cast me as one of the Lost Boys. When Mom came to see the musical, she got so upset over the depiction of the Native Americans that, from the stage, I could see her giving the principal a piece of her mind.

The mother starts flapping her arms as if she's swimming in the air. The girl rolls her eyes.

The other two girls who are friends have matching long black hair. I kind of want to name them Lisa and Laura, although I'm sure those are not their names and they aren't twins. I smile at them, and although they smile back at me, it's kind of a syrupy fake smile. The girl with the excited mom is Ayana and she says this is all her mother's idea. She would rather play tennis.

"Where are your parents?" Ayana asks, looking up at the bleachers. For a second I feel as if I should lie. Luckily, I don't get a chance to. Ili calls us to begin.

I wait my turn and go into the water. The first swimming station is easy. I can pretty much outswim everyone in my group, although "Lisa" and "Laura" pull in pretty close. The second station is also a breeze. Treading water is fun. As we progress to the other stations, Ili take notes and speaks to Renée. If they were giving out scores, I would be number one, or an easy number two.

"So, when do we do the ballet legs and flips and upside-down twirls?" I eye the high school girls in the water who are being tested on those very same movements.

"That takes a lot of practice," Ili says. "Think you got what it takes to be a Mermaid?"

"Me? I have no doubt. I'm part fish."

"Where's your guardian, so we can talk to them about you joining?"

I lose my smile right away.

"Um, my mom is waiting by the car in the parking lot. I'll give her the information."

I try my best to keep the papers dry as I shove them into my tote. I'm so going to be a Mermaid.

"I had a blast, didn't you?" I ask Daniel. Ayana cracks only a little bit of a smile. I think she liked it, too. Our group walks toward the locker room to change, including "Lisa and Laura."

"Do you think you'll join the team?" one of them asks Daniel. I don't like the way she sounds.

"Yeah, definitely," Daniel says.

"I don't think I've ever seen a boy do synchronized swimming before. Have you?" she asks her nosy friend. They shake their heads like they're synchronized swimming monitors. Daniel looks down at his tote bag. He's not upset, but I am because they're making him doubt himself. I can't stand here and keep quiet while they make him feel uncomfortable.

"What do you care if he's trying out for the team?" I say. "Are you some sort of artistic synchro expert? How many years have you done this?"

I bombard her with multiple questions, not really waiting for her to answer them. Who crowned her the queen of the synchronized swimmers?

"I wasn't talking to you," she says. What a lazy response.

"I'm talking to you. Me. My name is Nat, and his name is Daniel," I say. "And I would choose your next words carefully."

The girl doesn't know what to do with herself, so she backs off. She and her silly friend walk away.

"Whoa," Daniel says. "She was just asking a question."

"No, she wasn't. She was being mean."

"I don't need you to speak for me." Daniel walks away, too. I'm so confused. I thought I did the right thing. All signs pointed to those girls being total jerks. I guess Daniel's not used to having someone take his side.

I follow Ayana into the dressing room.

"I don't get it," I say.

Ayana just shrugs.

I can't help it. Mom says whenever someone acts out

of bounds, you need to school them. My technique could use some polishing, but who cares? I got my point across. Who said synchronized swimming is only for girls?

I change out of my swimsuit and go through the conversation over and over again. Did my loud mouth get the best of me? I definitely did not hit pause the way Ramón asked me to do.

"You were great!" Sheila gives me a hug when I join her outside in front of the facility. "Hey, what's wrong?"

"I thought I was helping someone out. Instead, he seems mad at me."

Sheila follows my gaze as I watch Daniel walk to his parents' car.

"Well, you have to let them get to know you first," she says. "Okay?"

Ayana's mother is signing the stack of papers, ready to give them to Renée. Ayana shakes her head at me. I kind of like Ayana. Then it dawns on me. The one thing missing from today's adventure is Joanne. I would have looked over to Joanne and she would have immediately understood why I had to put those girls in their place. It also makes me wonder, would Joanne like Daniel and Ayana?

To cheer me up, Sheila buys me tacos and a large horchata. It's the best-earned taco ever.

CHAPTER 7

It says it right there in bold letters. *Monthly fees. Competition fees. Accessories. Costumes. Caps. Noseclips. Glittering fee!* The list goes on and on. Also in bold, *Fees are subject to change.* Ouch.

Joanne puts aside the manga and picks up the handout I'm staring at. "So much money."

On a break from taking care of her baby cousin, Joanne came over to download what has happened since last I saw her. We've obviously been texting, but it's important to go over things in person.

"I guess the great synchronized swimming challenge is a bust," she says, and I'm so disappointed. As if I'm going to give up that easy. A challenge is a challenge, even if it was made by a rando guy who thinks I can't do it. I also wonder if maybe, just maybe, Joanne doesn't want me on the team. When I mentioned Daniel and Ayana, she seemed interested enough, but I watched her eyes flicker over to her manga.

"I'm not giving up. Maybe I can bring it up to my parents,"

I say. "If they sponsor me, I can make it happen."

The dream of being lifted during a synchronized swimming competition came to me again. This time I was performing in front of my whole school. Joanne was in the crowd and cheering so loudly. She pulled out a large banner that read NAT FOR SCHOOL PRESIDENT. SHE'LL TREAD FOR YOU!, which as a slogan didn't quite make sense, but still. Sheila says when she wants a certain expensive eye shadow, if she dreams about it, then it's meant for her to buy it. I think there's something to that.

"What should I do?"

Joanne furrows her brow. "You'll need a PowerPoint presentation on why synchronized swimming is for you."

"A PowerPoint presentation with slides and stuff?" I've never been so thorough when I ask for something.

She nods. We head over to my computer, open the program, and start. Joanne thinks I should keep it really short, about three slides. The focus should be on the benefits of being part of a team. I'm lucky Joanne is a total computer whiz, even though she doesn't have a computer of her own and usually just borrows mine.

We pull up images of Anita Alvarez with a video snippet of her Olympic performance. I add bullet points about how the water can have a calming effect. Joanne bolds the word *pause* in there.

"I'm so glad you're the smart one in this duo," I say. "I'll present it today."

"Now can we get back to what's important?"

The con schedule was released earlier. We have to figure out a plan.

"I still don't know what I'm going to wear."

"Nat! We don't have much time to coordinate." Joanne can be a bit intense when it comes to the con. I want to tell her to chill out.

"Joanne, what if my parents say yes to me? What if I add you to my presentation? What do you think?"

I want Joanne to be on the team. I don't want to recount my adventures after the fact. We can be a total force together.

"I don't really like swimming," she says. "Besides, my aunt was so happy with me taking care of baby Noah. She wants me to come over even more."

"Well, I think our next PowerPoint presentation should be on how you need to have a little fun this summer," I say. "There are child labor laws, you know."

"Not for my family."

Joanne is wrong. Swimming can totally be her thing. It can be *our* thing. There can be duets in our future with matching outfits. It would be awesome. Oh well.

We spend time looking over the schedule for the con. My homework is to decide who I will cosplay. I wonder if we'll ever outgrow dressing up, if there will be a time when we'll be too busy with other things.

I lie down on my bed. Joanne lies right beside me. It's

been a while since Joanne spent the night. Her parents don't really believe in allowing her to stay over. It took them meeting my parents to finally let her. They are way old-school. We lie like this, watching videos on my phone.

"I have butterflies in my stomach," I say. "I don't know about the presentation." I rub my belly to settle the butterflies down. Joanne, in support, rubs her belly, too.

"You can convince people way older than you to race you," she says. "And what if your parents say no? Would it be that bad?"

Would it? I literally discovered the sport only a couple of days ago. I don't have any connection to it at all. I'm being silly.

"This may sound corny, but for once I want to do something glamorous without it being a secret," I say. "For my parents to understand. Pretty things are pretty."

Joanne goes silent. "You know *you're* pretty. Right?"

"Oh yeah. I know I am." Mom and Dad always make sure to remind me. Even when I would get into fights because kids were bullying me, my parents made sure I was doing okay with my self-esteem, with affirmations and such.

Even with all that, there might be a tiny seed of doubt. I can't admit it to Joanne or to anyone. I don't know. Maybe if I'm on such a glamorous team, people will look at me differently. Maybe I won't be the hotheaded one. I'll be the synchro girl instead.

Joanne goes back to figuring out con things while I go over the presentation. Joanne and I stay like this for an hour, together but doing separate activities. Then I get this real fear: What if there will be a time when Joanne and I will no longer be interested in the same things?

Before she heads home, Joanne wishes me good luck.

"You got this," she says. I hope so. I walk back to my room to prepare.

In the living room, Mom and Dad are arguing, which is not a good sign. It's not like a drag-out argument like the ones I've heard from my neighbors Chucha and Bob. They're always at it, but I think it's just their normal way of talking. If they're not screaming at each other, I always assume one of them is sick or away.

My parents agree on most things, but sometimes they argue over methods. Today the topic is veterans being kicked out of their apartments after a millionaire bought up the building. Mom believes a call to action is imperative, shaming the owners in the media, the usual. Dad's approach is to find a mediator, to get the two parties together to find a solution.

"They need to vacate in less than two weeks. You're being ridiculous," Mom says. She prepares a large salad while Dad grills chicken.

"Your solution doesn't always yield results. In the meantime, they need a place to live." Dad raises his voice a bit.

Ramón joins the fray. He talks about boycotting everything the millionaire owns. Last year, Ramón led his classmates to walk out of school in protest of gun violence. Mom picked me up early from school and we joined the walkout. It was a whole family affair.

Mom eventually leans on Dad's broad shoulders. I like it when they're like this. Sweet. No confusing arguments to make my head spin.

This is it. I clear my throat.

"Wow! Aren't *we* dressed up!" Mom exclaims.

Joanne and I decided I needed to look professional. I wear the blazer from my short-lived Catholic school days. It doesn't really fit. My arms are too long. I'm also wearing a too-tight skirt. High-top sneakers in red completes the look. Oh, and a neon-orange headband.

"What's on your mind, Natalia de la Cruz Rivera y Santiago?" Dad loves saying my name, all five hundred parts of it. Each name given to me has a meaning. There's a framed chart in my room explaining their origins.

Well, here goes nothing.

"I have a brief presentation I would like to, uh, present."

Ramón, who is working at the dining room table, starts to laugh. Mom shushes him.

I pull out my laptop and take a large sip from my water bottle.

"Synchronized swimming began in 1891 and was first known as water ballet. Now called artistic swimming, the sport is very challenging and uses every part of the body. Not only must you be a great swimmer, but you must be flexible and have strength."

Mom and Dad listen intently. Even Ramón walks over to the living room to see what I'm talking about.

"The L.A. Mermaids is the only artistic swimming team in the city. The founder is Renée Williams, and she's been swimming since she was seven years old. Her mission is to make sure kids of all ages and ethnicities can learn synchronized swimming." I point to the image of the Mermaids and how it's a true representation of what a team should look like.

The presentation ends with a brief video of a routine. I made sure to select one of Anita Alvarez's duets that she performed at the Olympics. Both my parents clap, as does Ramón, when I'm done.

I hand them the papers with the multiple fees broken down. Mom and Dad look them over. I stand there sweating. It's too hot to wear a blazer, but now that I've committed to the fit, I don't think it's a good idea to take it off.

"Well, Nat, I'm really proud of what you've done here," Mom says. "I can tell you worked hard."

I nod. This is good. She likes my presentation. Joanne's idea is paying off.

"Me too, Nat," Dad adds.

"Let us talk about this and we'll get back to you with our decision," Mom says. She stands, signaling that the conversation is done.

"How long?" I ask.

"Excuse me?"

"How long do I have to wait for your decision?"

Mom gives Dad a hand as he gets up from the sofa. Mom doesn't like it when someone ask her for a time-table. Funny—everything I'm doing, I've learned from her. When I was doing poorly in my history class, she went over how I can approach the teacher with a deadline for handing in extra work. I guess she doesn't appreciate it when I'm doing it to her.

"How about we get back to you in a couple hours?"

I nod. Mom and Dad head to their bedroom and close the door. I can hear them tune in to the nightly news.

"You can take those clothes off. You don't look very comfortable," Ramón says. I shake my head. The professional attire might just be a deal breaker for the parents. Although the sweat is literally pooling down my sides, I want them to see I mean business. Ramón probably thinks I'm acting silly. What else is new?

I stand, holding my laptop by my side like a book. Instead of making jokes, Ramón hands me a cup of water. I didn't realize how thirsty I was. Public speaking is a lot of work. I don't know how my parents do it, especially Mom. I've seen her talk in front of hundreds of people, sometimes in two languages. It's impressive how she can captivate an audience and move them into action. I can only hope she sees this in me and I've moved them into giving me what I want.

It hasn't even been ten minutes. I guess I should sit down. Ramón places his pen down and pulls out a blank sheet of paper.

"You're stressed, so let's work through this. What happens if they say no?" He creates a column with a large NO on top. A second column has the word YES on it. "Go ahead and write how you would feel."

The list I make isn't very long. There's a line about how all the work of the presentation will have been wasted. There is also this feeling that perhaps Mom and Dad won't see it from my point of view.

"Now think what happens next. If you get a no, what are your next steps? If you get a yes, what then?" Ramón adds.

Time goes a little bit faster. Soon the two hours are up, and I stand. Eventually Dad steps out of their bedroom. Then Mom. They both have smiles, and this fills me with hope.

"Nat, we've discussed your presentation and looked over the papers," she says.

"And?"

"I'm sorry, Nat, we're going to have to say no," he says. "Mom and I feel that although synchronized swimming is considered a sport, it overly emphasizes presentation."

My face drops. I thought for sure it was going to go my way.

"We don't like how body-conscious this sport is, especially when it comes to image," Mom says.

"That's not what the team looks like. If you noticed in slide two, you can see how different everyone is. Size doesn't matter. We are all healthy."

"This may be true, but the national organization on the whole perpetuates a stereotype where only a certain type of girl is allowed to shine," she says. "And that person is usually thin and white."

"Just because an organization is off doesn't mean it's all bad. What if I can change the way things are done? Aren't you always saying we can be the change?"

Dad walks over to me and places his hand on my shoulder.

"We're proud of you for trying, but for now we are going to stick to our answer," he says. "Anybody want some tea?"

And just like that, my proposal to join the synchronized

swimming team is shot down. Ramón mouths the word *sorry*. I can't believe it.

I go to my room. Although I want to slam my bedroom door, I don't. It's not how we do things in this family. I'm so bummed out. I thought the presentation was perfect. Why can't they see how much I want to do this?

But wait a whole minute.

Dad *did* use the words "for now," as in maybe later they will change their minds. I look at the list I made with the help of Ramón. My parents won't sponsor my dream right at this moment, but that just means I'll have to find another way to convince them.

CHAPTER 8

If there's one thing I've learned from being a part of this family it's that when one door closes, you shove yourself against that very same door and bang it. Kick it. Scream until someone opens it. Okay, maybe this is not necessarily true, but it is what I'm taking away from my PowerPoint presentation fail.

I'm treading at the far end of Roosevelt Pool. I never realized how much treading works the legs and stomach. Treading kind of helps me think. I spent most of last night angry at Mom and Dad. They can be so set in their ways, even when they believe what they're doing is for the best. I understand exactly why they said no. Synchronized swimming promotes this ideal beauty, similar to what is found in fashion magazines. Thin girls who are light-skinned, and no Indigenous girls or fat girls. No one who looks like me. Even Anita Alvarez doesn't look like me.

Yup. I totally get it.

Will this stop me from finding a way to get on the team?

No. The first practice for the L.A. Mermaids is on Saturday. If I want to be a part of the team, I will have to make it to practice. I'm going to have to prove to my parents that they're wrong. Synchronized swimming can be for me. I just don't know how. So for now I'll keep treading water until an idea pops into my head.

Christian, the pool manager, gives me a nod.

"Looking good, Nat," he says.

Now that my pool ban has been lifted, I'm back to my regular headquarters. Christian made me promise to cool it, and I said I would. I still like Christian. It's hard to be mad at a person when you know they're right. I was wrong in attacking that boy. I'm trying to apply this same outlook to my parents, but I can't. Not yet anyway.

Joanne has her nose glued to a manga while Sheila talks to a boy who must be telling her jokes, since she can't stop laughing. As for me, my legs are getting tired from treading. No ideas emerge. I pull myself out of the water and plop down next to Joanne.

"How does she do it?" I ask Joanne.

"Do what?"

"How does Sheila manage to not curse these boys out every time they come over to her? I would charge them if they came up to me to ask stupid questions."

"I don't know," Joanne says. "Sheila doesn't seem to mind."

Sheila's laughing, but something about the way she

grins makes me think she's putting on a show. Mom made me watch a documentary about code switching—how we talk and act differently around certain sets of people. Sometimes we have to hide how we really feel. Deep in my gut, I feel Sheila's smile is fake and she really doesn't want this boy to talk to her.

I walk over to them. The boy ignores me and continues with his story, which doesn't surprise me.

"Sheila, I need to talk to you," I say.

"She can't right now."

Oh no, he did not answer for her. Christian stares at me from his office, and I know my next action will be a very important one. I take a deep breath. I remember the meditation app. I count to five, very slowly.

"Excuse me, Sheila, can I have a word with you?" I say. "In private, please."

Sheila rolls her eyes, but she still gets up and moves away from him.

"What is it?" she asks, but not in an annoying, you-are-interrupting-me kind of way. In fact, she seems a bit relieved.

"I need to figure out how I'm going to join the team," I ask. "I need your advice."

"You can't be serious. Your parents said no. I'm not getting involved. My job is to get you to Roosevelt Pool and back. That's all I'm doing."

Now she sounds annoyed.

"We should be heading out," she says. "Go get changed. I'll meet you by the front entrance."

Oh well—I tried.

Joanne and I change out of our swimsuits and walk over to Sheila, who doesn't notice us at all. Instead, she's concentrating deeply on a piece of paper.

"What's that?" Joanne asks.

Sheila covers the note and puts it in the back pocket of her cutoff jeans.

"Mind your business."

"How rude!" I say, and then I make the ugliest face I can muster. Joanne tries to top my face. Then we decide we'll walk with these ugly faces all the way home.

"Will you both stop?"

"What do you mean?" It's hard to answer with the ugly face, but we continue. If anything, Joanne and I are committed. We start singing a song—or try to, anyway. Sheila shakes her head.

"You two are ridiculous."

"I think Sheila has an admirer," Joanne whispers to me. An admirer? She's so old-fashioned. I bust out laughing and break my ugly face.

"You mean *admirers*. I bet she has a stack of love letters hidden in a secret compartment in her room underneath all her awesome Fenty makeup."

Joanne ponders this. "Is that where you would hide love letters?"

I have no idea. I've never had to worry about love letters. I'm too busy figuring out my life to be wondering who likes me. There are so many girls in my class who talk about kissing. Who has time for that? It's not to say that Joanne and I don't have our crushes. We definitely do, just not anyone real, mostly anime crushes.

"I would commit my letters to memory," Joanne says.

I try not to laugh. Joanne is such a die-hard romantic. She doesn't like to talk too much about it, but she writes fan fiction about her favorite manga character. One time she let me read a post, and it was all staring into each other's eyes and long, gushy kisses. I started reading the posts out loud, but Joanne got really embarrassed. She's never allowed me to read her posts again, which is too bad. Joanne's a pretty good writer.

"Bye," Sheila says.

We've arrived in front of Joanne's home. Because her parents aren't there yet, Joanne will go to the upstairs apartment, where her cousin lives, and help them prepare dinner. At least she has the rest of her day figured out. As for me, I'm nowhere close to solving my synchronized swimming dilemma.

"So, Sheila, what do you say we go over to your house and eat?"

Waiting at home are more of Dad's vegetarian delights, but I crave food that will stick to my stomach and help me think. Aunt Lupe never disappoints. Ever.

"Fine," she says, but she's not really paying attention to me. Sheila has this smirk. I bet she's still thinking about that letter. At least someone is having a good summer. I, on the other hand, am stuck at Roosevelt Pool.

Sheila's house is so different than mine. When you walk into Sheila's house, you see an oversized glamour shot of her mother, Aunt Lupe, taken not too long ago and hanging on the living room wall. Aunt Lupe is wearing heavy makeup and a captain's hat, like she's on a yacht. The picture has a sort of soft glow to it. I love it so much. Sheila thinks it's tacky. I can't wait to be old enough to spend money on professional photographs done for my fortieth birthday.

"Hi, Aunt Lupe." I greet her with a kiss. She's wearing a tight dress and heels. Mom always dresses professionally, mostly in suits. When she doesn't, she wears comfortable jeans and a flowy top. She doesn't like to accentuate her body too much.

"What? No food in your house?" Aunt Lupe teases. "Your mother never feeds you."

"She feeds me, but I like your food better," I say. Mom and Aunt Lupe are kind of competitive when it comes to who's the better mom. Aunt Lupe doesn't approve of how Mom is always out and about and Dad is the one who takes care of us. She's old-fashioned that way.

My aunt's laugh is deep and raspy. There are so many pictures of her throughout the house. A real glamour

Latina. And Sheila gets all her looks from her. I wonder what it must be like to wake up seeing so many pictures of her mom.

Every year, Aunt Lupe throws a big party to celebrate her birthday in the backyard. She likes to go all out with decorations and food. She even hires a DJ. We go every year and dance all night long. It's fun to see Aunt Lupe and my mom holding hands and dancing with each other. Mom says Aunt Lupe taught everyone in the neighborhood how to dance. She's even taught me some moves.

Sheila pours herself a tall glass of Coca-Cola. "Can I have some?" I ask. I lunge for the beverage before Sheila can answer, which causes it to spill on her shorts.

"Nat!"

"Sorry!"

"Hand them to me. I have a load I need to start," Aunt Lupe says. "Go on. Take them off."

Sheila goes to her room and returns with the wet shorts. Aunt Lupe walks over to the laundry room.

And that's when it all falls apart.

Aunt Lupe storms back, her face transformed into a blotchy red mess filled with rage.

"Who is this?" she yells. In her hand Aunt Lupe holds the piece of paper I saw Sheila staring at earlier today. I can barely make out what it says. Sheila doesn't say anything.

There are three things my aunt won't tolerate:

1. Don't ever change the channel when she's watching her telenovela, even if she's not in the room.

2. There is no such thing as gourmet tacos. There are only tacos, and the best ones are the ones that are made by her mother and her grandmother. Everything else is a lie.

And 3. Sheila will not, never, no way, ever have a boyfriend while she is living under Aunt Lupe's roof. Not until she's twenty-one years old, and maybe not even then.

"Who is writing to you about how beautiful your lips are, how they want to kiss them?" She stops and her eyes go even wider. The veins on her neck pulsate.

Sheila can't even open her mouth to defend herself. This proves a theory I've had for a while: Sheila is great with makeup and clothes, but she can't navigate touchy situations like this one right here. I have way more experience because, well, I'm always getting in trouble. You have to be quick on your feet.

"Thank you, Aunt Lupe. I was looking for that everywhere," I say, and take the letter from her hand. "I've never written a poem before."

Before she can say anything, I pull out my phone and find a picture of the manga character Sasuke Uchiha. Then I show it to Aunt Lupe.

"Joanne and I are planning to write at least four poems and mail them to him," I say. "I asked Sheila to make sure it didn't sound too corny. What do you think?"

Aunt Lupe isn't quite sure what to make of my story, but she also can't deny it. The thing is, I'm a strange girl to Aunt Lupe. She doesn't understand why my mom will let me attend some conference for cartoons that are not even in English.

"Does your mother know you're writing poems to a cartoon?" she asks.

I laugh because what else am I supposed to do?

"Why are you sending poems to him?"

"So they can send me an autographed picture of him, that's why. Then I can get a cheap frame and hang it on my bedroom wall."

"Ma, it's like writing to a celebrity." Sheila finally talks. She starts to caress my head, a total nervous reaction. I try to nudge her hands away from my not-combed hair, but Sheila ignores my signals. "It's what the kids are doing."

"I don't want any boy hanging around you. ¿Me entiendes?" Aunt Lupe says, her anger slowly fizzling.

"Ay, Mom. There are no boys," she says. "Please stop."

"I'm going to talk to Angela about these poems. Your mother needs to pay attention to what you're doing."

Eventually, Aunt Lupe goes back to the kitchen. Sheila wipes the sweat from her forehead. We eat the delicious meal in near-total silence.

"I better walk Nat home," Sheila says after dinner.

When we're far enough away from her house, I dig the poem from my tote.

"Do you mind?" Sheila says. Her palms are out, waiting for me to give the lovey-dovey letter back to her, but I don't. This letter is my ticket.

"You made me lie," I say.

"I didn't make you lie," Sheila says.

This is the funny thing about my cousin. I totally did her a favor, but for some reason she wants to act as if I'm at fault here. This is what is called misdirecting your anger. Or something. She's embarrassed by what happened, but she will come around.

Meanwhile, Sheila now owes me and I am preparing my ask. A plan is forming, and with each step we take, my mind revs up, placing the pieces together.

CHAPTER 9

"I want you to take me to synchronized swimming practice in Expo from now on," I say. "I'm joining the team."

Sheila refuses my request. She doesn't believe she owes me for saving her life. Her life! I'm going to remind her exactly what went down.

"Maybe I should go back inside and tell Aunt Lupe I was wrong," I say. "Who gave this to you? Was it that dork from the pool?"

"I won't say this twice," Sheila says. "Give me back the letter."

"No. Not unless you help me get to the synchronized swimming practice."

She shakes her head. If Sheila is afraid of her mom, she's doubly afraid of mine. Sheila's seen how my mother handles the cops. She doesn't want that smoke.

I grab Sheila's arm to try to get her to stop shaking her head no. I want her to really look at me. This is serious business.

"I know I'm always scheming. This is different," I say. "I just need you to take me to practice and back."

"How are you going to pay for it?"

This is the big question. Like any good entrepreneur, I already crunched the numbers. I have more than enough saved to pay most of the fees for the first few months.

"There's a scholarship I'm applying to." I found a grant given to young people doing sports. It's not much, but any dollar amount helps. I don't tell Sheila I'll have to forge one of my parents' signatures on the form. "I'm almost sure I can qualify."

"And if you don't?"

"Sheila, my summers are built on me making money. I can raise it if I have to."

She still shakes her head.

"What you're doing is called blackmail," she says. "I don't need to give in to your demands."

In order for me to be part of the team, I will need her help. That's all there is to it. She has to help me. Besides, I'm her favorite cousin. Actually, there's no actual proof I'm her favorite. In fact, there are days when I'm not sure if she even likes me, although we do spend a whole lot of time together. That has to count for something.

"All you have to do is get me to practice," I say. "Please. I really want this to happen. I can make it work."

After a few practices under my belt, I will eventually

invite my parents to a competition. I will win many medals, and they will realize how wrong they were. Mom will even grow to love the sequined bathing suit I will gloriously walk around in—while doing homework, while strolling through the neighborhood . . . It could totally happen.

Sheila flips her hair to the side. We're almost to my house. She'll have to make a decision soon. I can't tell which way she's leaning toward.

"If you do me this favor, I promise to be the best I can be. That means no fighting, no arguing, no nothing. Just me working out in the water. I swear to God."

"Ay, fine. I'll bring you to practice. Now give me the letter and shut up."

Yes! She's going to do it. I'm going to be an L.A. Mermaid. My Technicolor dreams are about to come true!

"You're doing what?"

Joanne is not exactly keen on me joining the team.

"Sheila is going to take me to practice."

"What happened with your parents?" she whispers although I'm in my bedroom and my parents are down the hall.

"They're not going to find out just yet, and when they do, they'll see how great I am. It will be too late and they will love it."

It'll be like in every feel-good film I've ever secretly

watched—secretly because Mom doesn't appreciate these unrealistic portrayals of the world. In a way I feel like I'm doing my parents a favor by withholding information. They'll be proud of how much of an initiative I took. It's elaborate, forging signatures and all, but I'm sure they will come around. What I don't get right now is why doesn't Joanne see this? This is good news.

"You said practice is over at Exposition. When will I be able to see you?" she asks. "You'll be busy."

I didn't think about this.

"You're babysitting, remember? We can spend Sundays together." Well, technically Sundays are reserved for my family, although I don't say as much to Joanne. "Besides, summer is just beginning."

To join L.A. Mermaids, there's a one-year commitment. Practice will be Wednesdays and Saturdays and will become more frequent when we get closer to competitions. My schedule will be busy, but there are pockets of free time in there.

"This summer is going to suck," she says.

Why can't Joanne be happy for me, happy at least for my scheme sort of working? I'm reminded of two summers ago. Mom and Dad were invited to Mexico to attend a fancy academic conference. They decided to turn the business trip into a family vacation with a full month of us visiting Mexico. I was so excited. When I told Joanne, she was so hurt. It was as if my parents had devised this whole plan to exclude her. When we returned, it took Joanne five full days for her coldness to thaw out. It wasn't until after I gave her a Mexican wrestling mask to match the one I got that the Joanne I love finally reemerged. I make a mental note to see what I can buy her to cheer her up.

"Why don't we make a list of the activities we want to do together this summer?" This idea comes from what Ramón had me do right before the synchro presentation fail. "Like what we do for the con. We can make a schedule."

Joanne hesitates, but she eventually pulls out a notebook and a calendar for us to look at. My schedule is pretty much set, we just have to block out the hours we can get together to create our costumes and have fun. After a while Joanne starts to relax, which means I relax, too.

"I hate taking care of that baby," she says.

"But he's so cute!"

Although honestly, her cousin Noah looks like a gnome with his scrunched-up face. He has the face of an old baby, if you know what I mean.

"Do you want to trade places with me, then?" she asks.

I should not be trusted with any living thing. It's why we don't have any pets. I had a goldfish once and I decided the fish needed to bulk up, so I overfed the poor thing and wondered why the next morning it was floating upside down.

"Joanne, this summer is going to be epic because we are epic. You'll take care of an old baby while making a couple of dollars. I'll get closer to fulfilling my dream as a Latina Esther Williams," I say. "It's going to be the best summer ever."

Joanne reluctantly agrees. This is an adjustment, but so is life. We will make it work. I'm sure of it.

CHAPTER 10

Things I notice as I walk to my first day of practice: I need a cap and a noseclip, and I'm definitely not wearing the right swimsuit. It's not to say I didn't have the list of items I needed to be a part of the team. I do. I just didn't have enough time to order things. Our local sporting goods store doesn't have what I was looking for. Who am I kidding? If I want to get to a sporting goods store, I would have had to explain to my family why and I couldn't do that. As for ordering it online, it would've taken too long. So my two-piece suit with my belly out is what I'm currently modeling.

I spot Ayana from tryouts.

"Hello," I say.

It doesn't surprise me that Ayana is decked out in the latest synchronized swimming gear, right down to mirrored goggles. Oh yeah, I forgot. I don't have fancy goggles, just ones I found at the 99-cent store ten minutes before getting to the pool.

"Where did you get those?" I say, pointing to her goggles.

"My mother," she says with a bit of a sigh. As if on cue, her mother rushes over to us and hands her a Hydro Flask. Ayana refuses to acknowledge her. I give her mother a polite smile.

"Mrs. Fekadu, parents aren't allowed on deck," Coach Renée says.

Ayana's mom becomes completely flustered, apologizes, and rushes back to the benches. Ayana might be annoyed, but I secretly wish my mom was as excited about synchro as Ayana's mom. When Sheila picked me up this morning, Mom was on her way to a meeting. She looked really polished in a blue dress. Her hair was up in a bun and she wore this bright red lipstick. Sometimes I play with her lipsticks (she doesn't own many, nothing close to Sheila's collection). I open the lipsticks and smell the tubes.

"You look pretty, Mom," I said. She leaned over and gave me a big wet kiss.

"Have fun at the pool, my fierce one," she said.

It hurts not being able to tell Mom. I want to share this with her so she can see how important it is to me. Isn't that what family is for, to share in the good times, not just the bad?

Sheila is inside, talking to Kim. She fulfilled her part

of the bargain. I sort of wish she would cheer me on or at least hold a towel out for me. Who knows how rough this practice will be?

Daniel runs toward the deck. He's late. From the look on Coach Renée's face, she's not happy. She stops talking and stares at him until he joins us.

"Uh-oh," I say.

"Now that everyone is here, one thing I will not tolerate is lateness. Yes, most of you are being driven here. Some are taking public transportation. It doesn't matter. To be an L.A. Mermaid, you must make a commitment to your whole team to make it to practice and competitions on time."

Daniel stares at his flip-flops. I look down and try to hide my sneaks, but it's too late. Renée noticed and is about to give us another speech, using me as an example of what not to do.

"You should have each received the list of what you are required to wear to practice. You can't come to practice in bikini tops. You must wear a racerback swimsuit, cap, and noseclip. Sneakers are allowed when we're doing our cardio, but you will need flip-flops to change into. Your hair must be secured in a bun or a tight ponytail."

I'm basically a checklist of what you shouldn't wear. I'm glad I'm not the only one. Younger kids wear frilly swimsuits with ruffles. Some have forgotten their flip-flops. Apparently, we will also need yoga mats to do our stretches on. There are so many things to remember.

Coach Renée pulls out a clipboard.

"Let's go over what practice will look like," she continues. "Every practice starts off with stretching followed by cardio. For some of you, this might be the first time you will be stretching. Stretching is critical. . . ."

I raise my hand.

"When will we be getting our sequined swimsuits?"

Coach Renée tilts her head. "That won't be happening until closer to our first competition, which will be in late September. We must work on the basics."

She hands out extra yoga mats. I try to show her how I can do a split, and she does a full stop.

"You do not immediately do a split. You warm your body up first."

Daniel raises his eyebrow. I guess Coach Renée is not the type of person who can be easily impressed. She's probably seen way too many splits.

Stretches. Stretch to touch your toes. Stretch your back. Stretch your arms. Stretch. Stretch. Stretch.

I never knew that stretching could feel like a workout. I'm sweating.

"You want a sip?" Daniel offers me water and I'm beyond grateful. I drink before Coach Renée notices how I failed to secure a water bottle, too.

"I'm going to die," I say.

"And we haven't even gotten into the water yet," he says.

"I thought it's called synchronized swimming," I say. "Not synchronized stretching."

Ayana snorts, which in turn makes Daniel laugh. Coach Renée glances over and we duck our heads, bending them toward our knees. Oh man, this is going to be rough. At least I can share my pain with Daniel and Ayana. The pool is so inviting and empty, tempting us to jump right in, and yet we're still not ready, according to the coach, who now tells us to start running.

We sprint back and forth. When we're done with that, we squat. Squats. Oh my god. How many squats can we do? Apparently 500 million trillion. My thighs scream in pain. My arms are about to laugh at my thighs when the coach asks us to raise our arms up while we squat. And when my legs and arms feel like jelly and can't possibly continue, the coach stops us and finally tells us to get ready to go in the water. Yes.

"Five minutes to get your cap on." Coach Renée demonstrates on an older swimmer how to put our caps on. She hands out caps to those who have not purchased them. Mine is hot pink. Lucky for Daniel, he doesn't need to wear one.

"Can you help me?" I ask him. It takes us three tries to get my big head and all my hair into the cap, but when we do, I feel so Esther Williams. I wish someone would take my picture, but there's no time for selfies, since Coach Renée is counting down.

Then I do what I normally do in a pool.

"Cannonball!" I scream at the top of my lungs.

"Natalia!"

Oh no.

"Out of the pool. Right now. You are not to jump into the pool like that. As a synchronized swimmer, you will be diving into the water. Like so."

On cue, one of the more experienced swimmers pulls herself out of the pool and does this amazing quiet dive. There is barely any splash.

"Try it," Coach Renee says. I climb out of the pool and do a dive. It looks nothing like what the other person did.

"Coach Yvette will be taking over practice. She's the novice coach this year. Pay attention to her instructions," Coach Renée says. "And welcome, new swimmers, to your first artistic swimming season!"

Coach Yvette is a tall brunette with a tattoo by her left breast. I can't tell what the tattoo is of, but I'm almost certain it's of a mermaid. Will everyone who joins the L.A. Mermaids be forced to get ink, because that would be amazing! I'm so ready. Before I can ask her if the tattoo is a requirement, Coach Yvette begins.

"You will be swimming one hundred and fifty meters; twenty-five meters equals one lap. We will be doing six laps," she says. "When you reach the end of the pool,

I want you to pull yourself out and do five squats. Call them out. Do you understand?"

We are doing laps. Laps upon laps. Swim from one end of the pool to the other end. Get out of the pool. Do five squats. Dive into the pool. Repeat.

"I don't hear you counting," Coach Yvette says.

"Maybe it's because I can barely breathe," I mumble.

"Me too," says Daniel.

"Save me," Ayana pleads.

The only two who seem to be more than happy with this torture are the two girls who had a problem with Daniel, "Lisa" and "Laura." Their actual names are Mayra and Olivia. They've been pretty much ignoring us, which is funny since we're on the same team. Maybe they're robots. Synchronized swimming robots sent to make sure we can hack this. Well, I can, so when it's time to yell out the number of squats, I scream as loud as I can. Too bad these drills are never-ending.

When are we going to do a ballet kick in the water? When will I learn how to twirl upside down in the water? I'm not sure how much longer I can take it. My legs are burning. My arms are on fire. When will this madness end? Just when I'm sure I'm about to fall apart, Coach Yvette makes an announcement.

"Good work. Gather around. I'm going to teach how to do a proper eggbeater," she says.

Amen to all that is sequined and shiny. Amen to Esther

Williams and Anita Alvarez. We're finally doing something that seems so very synchronized swimming. We learn how to rotate our legs to keep our bodies stationary and our upper body floating above the surface. Then she teaches us our first arm boost movement. As we eggbeat, we shoot our arms straight above our heads, then drive our arms back down to our sides, making sure to create a splash. Sure, it's not super intricate, but it looks great. We are all in a line, beating some eggs and boosting our arms.

Just when I master all there is to do with eggbeating and arms, Coach Yvette calls time. Practice is over. I swim over to the deck. It takes me a couple of tries to boost myself up from the pool. I'm so tired.

"Don't forget to drink lots of water and eat healthy foods."

I can only offer a nod to Coach Renée and Coach Yvette.

Ayana's mom races after her with a towel. Daniel and I slowly head to the changing rooms. It's not like I have much of a choice. My body is practically shutting down. Synchronized swimming is so hard.

"I really thought we were only going to do squats and stretching," I say to Ayana and Daniel.

"I don't know about you, but I can't imagine doing this for the next ten months," Daniel says.

Behind us I hear Mayra and Olivia giggle to each other. Not once do they talk to us or anything. They go off on their own to change in the bathroom. At least they're not being mean. Indifference is a type of meanness, though.

"Hey, every part of my body is in pain and it will probably be worst tomorrow, but we did it!" I say. "We got through our first practice. That's a big deal. There should be a parade celebrating us!"

Ayana chuckles.

"I don't know about a parade," says Daniel. "But I do know squats should be canceled."

Dad had a brilliant idea a while back. When I was struggling with English class, he made me create a group chat with two of my classmates. We would read each chapter and discuss afterward online. The cool thing about doing that was then I didn't feel so overwhelmed by the book.

"We should start a group chat. That way, we can help each other," I say. "I can send you videos on synchro and you can do the same. What do you think?"

Daniel doesn't even hesitate. He pulls out his phone and starts taking down my number. Ayana follows.

"What should we call ourselves?"

"That's easy," I say. "The Synchro Survivors."

Ayana shakes her head. "If I'm going to come here every week, I need an incentive. I don't want to *survive* anything."

I rack my brain.

"What about the Eggbeat This!" Daniel says. Although it definitely sounds slightly perverted, I kind of love it. So does Ayana, because she can't stop laughing. We make it official. Eggbeat This! it is.

"We need shirts."

"I think that's going too far. Okay, bye, see you online," Daniel says as he enters the boys' bathroom.

Ayana and I go into the girls' and change.

The first video I send to the Eggbeat This! chat is an Esther Williams GIF followed by fire emojis.

CHAPTER 11

El Mercadito is by far one of my favorite places. There are so many great things to buy: jerseys celebrating your favorite fútbol team, cowboy boots, toys you never thought you wanted. What really makes this place special, though, are the dueling mariachis working in the two upstairs restaurants. Not only do you get to eat tacos, burritos, and all the horchata your body can withstand, but mariachis will serenade you while you're chewing. Sure, mariachis are nothing new and the place is sometimes touristy, but I still love coming here.

My parents have been bringing the family to El Mercadito ever since Raymundo, my oldest brother, was a newborn. We celebrate graduations, birthdays, Mother's Day, Father's Day. You name the special day and you'll find us here talking loudly, since everyone in the restaurant must compete with the mariachi bands playing at opposite ends of the restaurants. My memories of this place are always filled with joy.

Not today, though. Today is different.

"No to colonization tactics!" Mom yells into the megaphone. Others join in with "Hell, no!" I'm holding a sign that says #CheapCathyHasGotToGo!

Earlier this week, a white woman got into an argument with one of the vendors here. She didn't like the price she was quoted for a cute Mexican dress. The lady decided to call the cops. The whole act was caught on tape. Online, people started calling her Cheap Cathy. When Ramón showed me the video, I got so mad. Why would anyone come to El Mercadito and argue over an already low price? Don't buy it, then!

There's a camera crew interviewing Mom. When they are done, Mom insists they speak to the vendor. I love seeing Mom in charge. Where there's injustice, Mom is right in the thick of it. She doesn't back down. In community meetings, she will take the microphone and argue with anyone. Don't let her soothing voice fool you. She will calmly use big words to quietly destroy the person and convert them into a puddle. Dad says I get my gift of never being afraid to speak to people from her.

"No to racism!"

"Hell, no!" I scream this because it is a rare moment when I can curse for a good cause. Most of my mother's friends are here with us. When you grow up attending marches and board meetings, you end up seeing the same people. The kids I ran around with in front of courthouses are now yelling out curses, too. We all are. Usually, Dad and Ramón join in, but they're having their date. Mom and me, this is our date.

"How are you doing?" Mom asks after she finishes with the interviews. I wonder what the name of her lipstick is. It's a soft mauve color. Sophisticated.

"I'm okay."

Honestly, I'm exhausted. Every single muscle in my body hurts, including the muscles in my fingers. I can't tell her this because she has no idea about practice. Sheila has kept her promise for the past two weeks. She's picked me up and taken me to Exposition Park. She's had the goofiest grin on her face. I guess the boy with the love letter is probably sending her more notes. Although Sheila still thinks I'm blackmailing her, she doesn't complain. Maybe my practice gives her more time to connect with her new boyfriend. Fine by me. I just want her to keep my secret a secret.

"We are almost done here. Half hour more, promise," Mom says. She caresses my cheek. The good thing about this demonstration is the feast we will surely be eating soon.

We chant for another solid hour. In my world, a half hour never means a half hour. Also, time with Mom never really means alone time. Every hour is somehow connected to her work. I don't know how I feel about it. I just accept it.

When we're finally done, we walk upstairs. The restaurants are buzzing with life.

"¿Qué quieres, mi amor?" I don't know how long I've known Gemma. She's been working at El Mercadito forever. Gemma said when I was really tiny, she would hold me in between taking people's orders. Although she's asking me what I want to order, she already knows the answer—a wet burrito. Gemma takes my order. Mom is busy talking to a family seated next to us. Sometimes it's hard to get her attention. I order huevos a la mexicana for Mom.

"I think that went well. Don't you?" Mom finally sits down beside me. "The interviews will help. They even had someone from NPR."

The mariachis haven't started playing yet. They will soon. People keep coming up to Mom to ask her a question or thank her for defending the vendor. It's hard having a popular mom.

"What was I saying?" she says after another person stops by our table. "So, how's my Natalia doing? What has your summer been like?"

I draw in a deep breath. I want to tell her how much I hate squats. There are new terms I'm learning: sculls, tucks, open strokes. I want to tell her about the different figures, too, like the crane and the barracuda. Instead, I take a large sip from my horchata.

"Not much," I say. "A lot of laps in the pool. Reading manga. You know, the usual."

Mom has a concerned face. Can she tell I'm keeping

something from her? I don't like lying. It's not what my parents taught me to do. This family is built on trust and the truth, however ugly and complicated that may be.

"You seem preoccupied. Is everything okay between you and Joanne?"

I haven't seen Joanne as much. Truth be told, I think it's taking a toll. I feel like her texts are angry. I make sure to text her every little thing going on in practice, but Joanne barely comments. It's hard to share something you love with someone who isn't a part of it.

"No, we're good. She's been taking care of her cousin. She's kind of busy."

"That must be hard on you," Mom says. "Is there anything I can do to help?"

Summer is going by so fast. In three weeks, we will be back in school. We'll be starting our last year of middle school . . . then high school. Things are really changing.

"I think I need new clothes," I say. "For the start of school."

Ever since I started synchro, I feel my body has changed. I'm not losing weight—I just feel stronger. Laps and eggbeating are sculpting my legs and arms. I guess Mom is noticing the changes, too, and this makes me nervous.

"I'll order you clothes. You're growing so fast. New clothes for the new school year. You must be excited."

"Thanks," I say. I concentrate on finishing my food.

"Nat, what's going on?" she says. "It's not like you to be so quiet. Is there something wrong?"

There's a pit in my stomach. It reminds me how this lie will gnaw at me if I don't tell her the truth. When school starts, practice will be shifted to after-school hours. Although Sheila is still on board to pick me up from school and take me, I haven't really shared this with Mom. But I don't have a choice.

"I think I want to keep swimming. Do you think it's okay for Sheila to take me to the pool during the week?"

Mom places her fork down.

"After school? What about your schoolwork?"

"If I start falling behind, I'll stop. Promise."

Coach Renée and Coach Yvette are really adamant the L.A. Mermaids do well in school as well as stick to our synchro obligations. When we're not practicing, they want us to stretch at home and work on our routines. Land drill is what they call it when you work on your synchronized swimming routine out of the pool. Pretty cool term. Every day when I complete my stretching exercises and land drill in my bedroom, I check in with the Eggbeat This! group to let them know I did it. We do this to keep ourselves accountable. Mom would totally like this. She would be proud, wouldn't she?

"Please, Mom. Sheila said she would take me."

"I don't like this. Sheila has things she needs to take care of, like her own schoolwork." Mom takes the napkin and lays it across her lap. "Every time I see her, she seems to be glued to her phone or putting more makeup on. I don't understand how Lupe lets her—"

"Mom, do you even like Sheila?"

Mom is totally taken aback. I didn't mean for it to come out so strongly.

"I love Sheila, just like I love my sister."

The mariachis begin to play. Mom has to raise her voice for me to hear her.

"Why are you so against her wearing makeup? I think she's pretty."

Mom lets out a long sigh.

"Sheila," she says, "like most girls I know, has the potential to do so much more. I get frustrated when the emphasis is placed on beauty instead of education."

It's funny when Mom says this, because she is gorgeous, as in camera-ready gorgeous. When she's on camera, she doesn't go wild with makeup. Everything is very tame. But so what if Sheila experiments with her looks?

"Some people aren't meant to get good grades," I say. "It doesn't have anything to do with Fenty."

Mom is not only confused, but she's also slightly angry. I'm yelling at her, but that's because the mariachis are playing a fast-paced song.

"Who is Fenty?" she yells back.

"It's makeup, not a person. Never mind. You always

say people pass judgment on us all the time. They think we're uneducated because of what we wear or where we come from. Sheila is presenting herself the way she likes. Isn't that a good thing?"

The song the band is playing ends and I'm left wondering why Mom is so hard on Sheila. I angrily take a sip from my horchata, when Mom touches my arm.

"You're right. I'm sorry. I am passing judgment. When I was young, my mother always insisted we look a certain way. I think Aunt Lupe does the same to Sheila. There are other ways to feel empowered," she says. "Let me think about swimming after school. Okay?"

After a long pause, her worry lines recede. "Remember this song?"

They are singing Vicente Fernández's "Mujeres divinas." When Dad wants to annoy us, he sings Vicente Fernández songs at the top of his lungs. He drives everyone bananas.

Mom starts to sing along, as do most of the families in the restaurant.

"C'mon, Nat. Let's hear that beautiful voice of yours."

I start to laugh. She knows I can't sing at all. Ramón is the musician of this family. And me? I don't know what I am. The one who argues? The one who fights? Soon I'll be able to say I'm the synchronized swimmer.

Eventually I join in. I can feel Mom is going to say yes to swimming and that means yes to my secret. It's only a matter of time before I'll be able to tell her what I've been doing these past few weeks. My parents will be proud of me. They will, I'm sure of it.

"Let's take a walk," Mom says after we both finish our meals.

We walk through the many stalls. The vendors give her welcoming hugs. One day I'm going to be like Mom. When I walk by, people will be happy to see me. They'll whisper, "There's the synchronized swimmer. Did you see her hold her ballet leg in the water? Did you see her boost? Isn't she so poised, so full of grace?"

We stop in front of an ice cream vendor.

"Thanks, Mom," I say when she hands me a cone. "This was a good date."

"It was. Sorry I've been so preoccupied. The start of fall always brings so many meetings. It doesn't mean I'm not thinking of you and your brothers every second of the day."

"I know, Mom."

I have this cool thought in my head. What if I got the local news to come cover the L.A. Mermaids' practice? Mom loves using the press to spotlight the good in the community. If Mom could see how synchronized swimming is an empowering sport and not belittling to women, she would have to support me. It's definitely something to think about.

CHAPTER 12

After stretching and completing hundreds of booty tortures, aka squats, I start to count down to when my body will touch the water. Even as the temperature starts to slightly dip for L.A., I can't wait to dive in. The shock of the coldness wakes every muscle. The best way to combat the sudden chill is to swim.

The other day Joanne asked me how it feels to be in the water. It's hard to explain. In the pool, I feel both weightless and strong. When I do a tuck, I bring my knees up to my chest while sculling. Sculling means I'm moving my hands quickly in the water to keep my body from traveling across the pool. I then push my head back, going into a flip underwater, scooping the water to help propel my body backward. I have to do this movement really slowly, without traveling. It's not easy. You have to concentrate on so many things. Making sure you're using your stomach muscles. That you're not splashing water. It's intense. Under the water I am able to accomplish so much. I feel invincible every time I learn to do a new position.

"Get closer!" Coach Yvette yells as we try to align our bodies as close together as possible. At this very moment, I'm not thinking about the lies I'm spewing to my family or how I forced Sheila to take me to practice. I don't think about how my anger gets the best of me or how I've gotten into someone's face because of what they've said. Even my teammates Mayra and Olivia don't annoy me as much in the water. No one does. In here, I can make my body do amazing things.

Synchronized swimming is way better than the meditation app.

"Good job, everyone!" Coach Yvette says. "Come over to this side."

We all swim to her.

"Our first competition, the Irvine Classic, is coming up in two weeks, Sunday after next," says Coach Yvette. "Before you leave, make sure to pick up the agenda. It will have the information you'll need to attend."

"Where's the competition?" I ask.

"Irvine, silly. It's in the title," she says. Unlike Coach Renée, Yvette is way calm. I think it's because we're the babies on the team. She has more patience. Coach Renée is stricter with the older swimmers.

Irvine. Is there a bus to Irvine? How am I going to convince Sheila to take me?

I raise my hand again.

"Wait. Did you say the competition is on Sunday?"

"Yes. It's on a Sunday, September 17. You will have to be there with your hair gelled by seven a.m.," she says. "As you know, lateness will not be tolerated. If you miss a day of practice any time in the next two weeks, you will not be allowed to compete. It's important that everyone is here."

"Will we be having any extra practice?" Mayra asks.

"Maybe. We share Expo with water polo teams and other swimming teams. We'll have to see the availability of the pool."

Coach Yvette answers other questions. What to eat before the competition. How to dress. Making sure we wear our team colors of green and gold. In my head, all I keep thinking is, *How am I going to pull this off?* Sundays are family days. We are meant to be together. On the random Sunday we have obligations, Mom and Dad join in on them. There are so many obstacles to overcome, I can't think straight.

When the team is dismissed, I gather my yoga mat and bag. There's so much to figure out.

"Nat, can you hold up?" Coach Yvette calls out to me. "I want to speak to you."

I pray I'm not in trouble. I can't handle any other surprises right now.

"I wanted to talk to you about a couple of things. I noticed you haven't ordered your team bag and uniform yet," she says.

I haven't had a chance to order the items because being on the team is really tearing into my savings. I need to make more money to pay my dues and still have spending money for the con in October. All these little costs for the team are adding up so quickly.

"I've also noticed we haven't received an email address for your parents so we can keep them up to date on team events," she continues. "Can you text me that information now?"

I have to think fast. There is no way they can communicate with my parents. No way.

"My parents don't believe in emails."

Coach Yvette doesn't believe me, but she can't say that without offending me. My parents can be the type of people who don't own a computer or a cell phone. It happens.

"That's fine, but it would be great for you to bring them in so we can meet. I want to let them know about all the great things you're doing."

It won't happen. Not yet.

"Sure. I'll tell them to come by."

Being an L.A. Mermaid was supposed to be a place where I can feel stress-free. I guess that only works in the water and not on land. On land I'm reminded that this plan will eventually blow up in my face.

"Is everything okay at home and school? If your responsibilities with the L.A. Mermaids are becoming too much, let's find a solution together."

I don't know how to break it to Coach Yvette. The strange thing is that ever since I started with the team, I've been able to concentrate more in school. My schedule is jam-packed. I don't have any free time to fool around, which means I can only focus on getting my homework done. I also don't want my parents to question this extra work once I tell them I'm part of this team. It's important that I can do all the things I'm meant to do, just like Mom. She's able to attend meetings, work her full-time job, and go out on dates with me. If she can do that, so can I.

"Everything's good. I have to go. My cousin is waiting."

Coach Yvette lets me go and I let out a sigh of relief. There's so much to plan. I need to get on it.

"Oh, and, Nat, the competition suits are coming in next week."

My grin can't be any wider. It's practically hurting my face. It's what I've been waiting for since day one. The sequined glam swimsuit. We finally get one. *I* finally get one. I've been dreaming about the suit ever since I first saw the L.A. Mermaids swimming at the Roosevelt Pool back in June. That seems so long ago, and here I am. I'm an L.A. Mermaid. Once the suit is on my body, I know the countless schemes and plots will be worth it, because who will deny me in my glittery awesomeness? No one.

"So, did you get in trouble?" Olivia asks when I arrive at the changing rooms. I'm almost certain she's hoping I am in trouble. Mayra and Olivia aren't complete jerks, but still there are moments when I'm sure they would rather not have me on the team. When we line up together, we're definitely an odd bunch of swimmers. Daniel is really tall. Ayana somehow gives Wednesday Addams vibes even without makeup or her usual all-black fit. And then there's me. The short fat girl. Mayra and Olivia make sense. They're about the same height. They're thin. Identical twins minus the color of their skin. They do everything synchronized, even talking to me right now. Olivia may be asking the question, but Mayra stands right behind her with her head tilted to the side, just like Olivia.

"I didn't get in trouble."

Is there a bit of disappointment on their faces? I don't care what they think. I'm going to keep showing up and showing out.

"What did Coach want?" Ayana asks.

"Well, we're finally getting our costumes next week!" I say, to shift the drama away from me. Everyone loves this. Olivia and Mayra start talking about the colors they hope our costume has. The music we'll be dancing to is a song from the musical *Hamilton*. The costumes are meant to reflect the song.

"I can't wait!" says Mayra. Olivia and Mayra hold each other and start jumping up and down like they won the lottery. I want to join in their party, but Ayana and I do what we usually do: stare at them until they stop.

"What are you going to do, Ayana?" Olivia says. "You'll have to gel your hair and wear a headpiece."

"What are you talking about?" I ask. Coach Yvette mentioned this earlier, and I'm totally lost. I keep imagining grabbing a jar of jelly and rubbing it into my hair, which doesn't seem right.

"You have to buy Knox gelatin so your hair doesn't move during competition." Olivia pulls out her phone and shows me a video of a synchronized swimmer gelling her hair. My heart kind of sinks. Gelling is just another reminder of all the things I have to learn in less than two weeks.

"They take points off if you don't. For presentation." Mayra gives me the once-over. "It's not just about who can hold their ballet leg up the longest."

This is a jab. Out of our team of five, I'm the only one who can float on her back and lift one leg straight up, all the while sculling to keep from moving across the pool. Once at practice, Coach Yvette timed us to see how long we could do it. Mayra and I were the last ones sculling. My leg was burning. but I kept at it. Eventually Mayra gave up.

"Not a problem," I say.

"We're going to be there with our hair gelled, our headpieces secured on our heads, and the biggest smiles ever," Ayana says. She also gives them the scariest grin ever. Ayana can really tap into her ghoulish side. Olivia laughs, but Mayra doesn't, which is too bad because it's funny. I finish changing out of my swimsuit and head out.

Daniel waits by the entrance for his mom to pick him up. Ayana and I wait with him while her mother is busy chatting up the coach with the usual multitude of questions she seems to have after every practice. Ayana is used to it by now.

"Did you hear?" I say. "They said our costumes will be ready next week."

"Cool," Daniel says. "Do you think they will sequin my shorts?"

"They better. One of the Evil Twins said they judge on presentation," I say. "If we're getting sequins, you better be getting sequins, too."

"Extra sequins," Ayana says.

"So many sequins, Disney will call and ask us to lead their electrical parade," Daniel adds.

"So many sequins that space aliens will beam down and ask us where we shop," I say.

We can't stop riffing off this by adding more sequin lines and laughing at how ridiculous they are.

"Bye, Evil Twins."

Olivia and Mayra walk past us.

"See you losers next week," Olivia says. Even with the name calling, Olivia and Mayra still wave goodbye to us.

"I'm not sure how I'm going to get to Irvine," I say. "It's not like the train will get me there by seven a.m."

"Why can't you just ask your parents to drop you off?" Daniel asks. "Oh, wait. How long do you think you can keep this thing under wraps? It's your first competition. Don't you want them to be there to cheer you on?"

"I'm going to tell them, just not yet. I want everything to be perfect."

"You can spend the night at my house," Ayana says. "My mom would be so happy to gel two girls instead of one. She probably won't be able to contain herself."

"Are you sure?" It's funny to see Ayana be nice when her go-to is always grumpy.

"I'm not doing this as a favor to you. I need a buffer. Look at her."

We turn to her mother giving Coach Yvette an earful. She's way more excited about our first competition than the whole team combined.

This might just work. My first competition, plus sequins for days.

CHAPTER 13

"Where exactly did you meet Ayana?" Dad asks. He's eating an omelet that's stuffed with vegetables but missing extra cheese. The even sadder part? I'm eating it, too.

"We met at the pool this summer. Remember?"

The competition is in two days. I've avoided telling my parents because I couldn't figure out the best way to approach the subject, so I decided that being casual about the whole thing might work. Also, I don't have a choice. I need to be at Ayana's house tomorrow.

Mom enters the dining room with her glasses atop her head. She's been working on a speech she has to give for the reopening of a community center. Ramón is set to play with his band. A free gig, he says, for exposure again—since they are breaking in a new lead singer.

"What do you think? She won't be here for our Sunday family time," Dad asks Mom, who is immersed in writing notes in her fancy journal.

She looks up after scribbling a super-long sentence.

"Oh, I don't like the sound of this. We try not to schedule anything on Sunday."

"I'll be home by dinner. I promise."

"And schoolwork?"

"I'll finish my homework tonight. I'll show it to you. I just need someone to drop me off at Ayana's house. She lives by USC."

"We haven't even met her parents," she says.

"Dad, you can meet her mother when you drop me off. Ayana is an only child. It's just her parents and Ayana. And Ayana's father is away, so it will be just Ayana and her mom. Please."

I'm begging. They have to let me go.

"I really can't handle this now," Mom says to Dad. He leans over and gives her a kiss.

"Don't worry. You do your thing and we'll manage. Right, Nat?"

Yes. This situation just got easier. I can make this work. I know I can. Dad's not as strict as Mom. Once he meets Ayana's mom, he'll be fine. I just need to make sure their meeting lasts only for a second.

I'm running to my room to get my overnight bag ready when there's a knock on my door.

"I'm busy," I say.

"I got something for you," Ramón says.

I shove my swimsuit gear into the oversized tote before opening the door.

"This was in the mail." He holds a package in his hand. I grab it and try closing the door.

"What's that you got there?" He nudges inside.

"None of your business."

Ramón places a hand over his heart, pretending he's injured. He even falls across my bed.

"You really should clean your room." He grabs a pile of shirts and hands it to me.

"I don't have time for this. I got homework to do and I need to pack."

"Sheila told me what you've been doing."

I drop the clothes to the floor. My heart thumps out of control.

"I think it's cool you're going after what you want, but you've got to tell Mom and Dad," he says. "This sneaking around won't work."

"How long have you known?" I ask.

"Nat. Sheila told me the day you asked her," he says, so matter-of-factly. "She doesn't want to get in trouble and you shouldn't be putting her in that position. It's not on her to carry your secrets. Sheila has her own."

He must be talking about the love letters. It doesn't matter. Sheila agreed to take me. She hasn't complained once since we've started practicing over at Expo.

"It's not like she doesn't get paid."

Ramón stands up from the bed. "Just because some-one gets paid to do your bidding doesn't mean it's the right thing. You have to tell Mom and Dad. What are you so afraid of?"

Doesn't he know? Hasn't he lived in this house long enough? Wasn't Ramón there when I made the big presentation and they both said no?

"They already said no to me."

Ramón shakes his head. "This isn't the way you do things. You might not like the reasons why they said no to you, but going behind their backs won't make them change their minds. How long do you think you can keep this up before you get caught?"

I throw myself in the middle of the mess. He's right.

"I just want to be a synchronized swimmer," I say. "Why is that such a crime in this family?"

Ramón scoots next to me.

"Remember when I told them I wanted to start a band? Mom thought it might take too much of my time, that I wasn't ready for the responsibility. I think she secretly believed it was just a phase, and maybe she was right in thinking that at first. But I proved to them music is something I love. You have to do the same, but not by lying."

"Are you going to tell on me?"

"No. *You're* going to tell them," he says. "Who knows? They might surprise you."

He's right, but it's all about timing. If they see me with the team, in all my sequined glory, they won't be able to deny how awesome synchronized swimming is.

"I promise to take care of it. Just give me a couple of weeks."

"Okay, but you better do it or I'm going to do it."

Before he leaves, Ramón turns around. "Good luck this weekend."

I go back to packing my stuff. There's so much pressure on my shoulders. I don't like the way it feels. It's different from figuring how to get money for my yearly con. When I was scheming ways to beat people at the pool, although I wasn't necessarily telling my parents what I was doing, I didn't feel I was doing anything completely wrong. I was competing with other kids. But this plan involves too many people. Sheila. Joanne. My coaches at the L.A. Mermaids. Now Ramón. Even my Eggbeat This! crew. It's not a matter of how I'll get through this. It's a matter of how I'll get through it with the least amount of damage.

"Earth to Nat."

It's Saturday and Dad has been telling me what I think is a funny story about when he was dating Mom. I can't keep track of the details because my head is bursting with so much. I can't actually handle another story crammed in there.

"Sorry, Dad. What did you say?"

"The one thing I can always count on is you having some sort of adventure," he says. "Ever since school started and you've been swimming after school, you've been a little too quiet. What's going on?"

"Maybe I'm just being a good student?" The fact that I end this statement like a question doesn't really help me. I look at the Google map. We're almost there. Ayana promised to meet us in front of her house.

"You have to make a left here."

When he does, Ayana's mom is outside with her arms crossed. Ayana is next to her, also with her arms crossed. They are so alike, even if Ayana wears black while her mother is in a lime-green shirt and jeans.

Dad pulls into the driveway. Ayana's mom is eager to greet us. I pray she doesn't say anything about the competition. Ayana promised she would pipe down. I've never actually seen Mrs. Fekadu be quiet. Sure enough, before Dad can even step out of the car, Mrs. Fekadu is by his window.

"It's so nice to meet you! Your daughter is an excellent swimmer."

Dad smiles while Mrs. Fekadu shakes his hand so vigorously, he doesn't know what to do.

"She is a good swimmer," he says.

"Mom, let's go inside," Ayana says.

Mrs. Fekadu ignores her daughter.

"Why don't you come in? Have some tea?"

"Dad has to go," I interrupt.

"Nat!" Dad scolds me. "Thank you for the invite, but it looks like Nat wants this old man out of her hair."

"We'll make sure to take care of her! If you want, I can send you pictures while at the competition."

"Sure."

I'm going to throw up. I watch with horror as Mrs. Fekadu takes down his cell phone number.

"Have a good time, Nat," he finally says. "Thank you for taking care of her."

Dad leaves, and I'm just glad their encounter went surprisingly well.

"We're so happy to have you here!" Mrs. Fekadu exclaims. "I hope you're hungry. You don't have any allergies, do you? You eat meat, right?"

"Mom, will you let her breathe?"

Ayana leads the way inside. The first thing I notice is a beautiful framed photo of Mrs. Fekadu and her husband on what I think is their wedding day. Mrs. Fekadu doesn't wear white. Instead, her gown is way more pretty than any wedding dress I've ever seen. I'm in complete awe of it.

"When was this taken?" I ask.

"In Ethiopian culture, the wedding is a week-long celebration. This picture was taken during Meles, which is held on the second day." Mrs. Fekadu looks so stunning. Her makeup is flawless, and she has on an elaborate crown and cape.

"What are you wearing?"

"Oh yes, it's called the Kaba. It's traditional in Ethiopian culture to wear it on your wedding day. Do you like it?"

"I love it."

My parents didn't believe in a big wedding. Instead, they went to the courthouse and got their marriage license. Mom wore a really simple dress, while my father was in jeans and a shirt. They don't have a picture framed in the living room, like the Fekadu family. They just have a small picture on the refrigerator of them kissing at the courthouse. Mom didn't even wear lipstick. Yet they both are so happy in the picture and so in love. I guess there's no one way of being pretty on your wedding.

Ayana grabs hold of my arm and leads me to the kitchen.

"Let's eat because we have to gel our hair before we go to sleep."

Everything smells so good. To say Ayana's mother knows how to cook is an understatement. I love everything Mrs. Fekadu places in front of me: juicy sega wat, a spicy chicken stew. Bowls of lentils and vegetable. I can't stop eating.

"If you ever want to eat Ethiopian food, you can always go to Little Ethiopia," Ayana says while finishing off her plate with injera, a type of spongy bread. "It's not as good as Mom's cooking, but it's close enough."

After dinner, we help clear the table and Mrs. Fekadu sets up our gelling station. She has a box of Knox, a kettle with hot water, a comb, bobby pins, and a hairnet to keep our hair in the world's most perfectly shellacked buns.

Mrs. Fekadu does my hair first, securing it in a really tight bun. There's a timing thing to gelling, since she has to mix water with the Knox and then comb it over our hair to create a superglue that keeps each strand in place. The water can't be too hot, or it will burn the scalp, or too cold, since the gel gets hard quickly if it is. When she's done, I feel like a mannequin. No movement in my hair at all.

Then it's Ayana's turn. Ayana has a lot more hair to work with and she is not happy at how her mom is shoving in one bobby pin after another.

"Ouch!" Ayana yells after Mrs. Fekadu pulled too hard.

"Oh, I'm so sorry," she says. "I just want to get this right. I didn't mean to hurt you."

Mrs. Fekadu stops what she's doing and gently rubs Ayana's neck. "Are you okay?"

"Yes, I'm okay, Mom." Ayana gives her mom a quick hug, which is kind of surprising to see. Ayana might be annoyed by her mother at times. Her mom can be a bit much, but she's also very loving and just plain nice. I think Ayana knows this, too.

"My mom would hate this so much," I say. "She would be ready to fight the synchronized swimming alliance, or whatever they're called, about placing Knox on our hair. I mean, what even is Knox?"

The more I think about it, the more I feel justified in not telling Mom.

We send Daniel pics and a video of the whole process.

I almost send it to Joanne, but I stop myself. I don't want her to feel left out. It's not that we've grown apart. I text her every single day. I just try to separate my synchro friends from Joanne. She would like Ayana as much as I do. Still, every time I bring up something new I learned at practice, Joanne doesn't really say much.

"You girls need to head to bed," Mrs. Fekadu says when she's finally done.

"Ayana? How will we sleep with this stuff in our hair?" I ask.

"I don't know. This is by far the worst experiment ever."

We talk throughout the night. I'm too nervous to sleep. Esther Williams and Anita Alvarez must have felt the same way before competitions.

When Ayana finally falls sleeps, I go over our synchronized swimming routine in my head.

CHAPTER 14

We arrive so early at the pool in Irvine that it's still dark out. Mrs. Fekadu steps out of the car to try to locate our teammates. She greets other early bird parents and introduces herself, pointing back to us. She's so different from my mom, but when it comes to intensity, they're not that different after all. They're both social butterflies even before the sun comes out!

"How does she do it?" I ask, unable to contain my deep yawn.

"I didn't tell you? She's not human."

We see Daniel, who is surrounded by his sisters. They're super cute and full of energy. Ayana and I grab our stuff and walk over to where the team is gathering.

I look around. There are a lot of girls here with extremely gelled buns and tracksuits, sleepy, and totally sizing each other up.

"Good morning!" Coach Yvette is so upbeat. She holds a tall cup from Starbucks. Mrs. Fekadu wanted to stop there to get coffee on our way. I explained to her how my family is boycotting the chain after a store kicked out high school kids for being "rowdy." She nodded and said she understood.

"No eating from McDonald's," Coach Yvette calls out to one of the intermediate swimmers. "Right?"

My stomach growls at the mention of McDonald's, but Dad insists on boycotting that place, too. Our weakness is In-N-Out, and now I'm hungry for that, too. So hungry. I ask Ayana for a granola bar and she gives me one. It's no burger, but I eat it.

One of the parents set up a large canopy. This will be our home base. Mayra and Olivia finally arrive with their mothers. They huddle together.

As I walk to the bathroom, I get a good view of the other teams. Their canopies are way more organized and elaborate. They have large banners hanging off their tents, announcing the names of their teams. The Aquababies. The Aquanuts. Everything Aqua. Some of the teams have a table set up for food and snacks— gallons of water and buckets of ice filled with bottles of Gatorade. Girls line up their yoga mats neatly in a row.

I can't help but notice that they kind of look the same. They're mostly white. They might have a couple of girls of color on their team. One brown or Black girl. Maybe. Definitely no boys.

Our canopy is kind of old. The parents at today's competition aren't wearing matching colors. Our yoga mats are not neatly lined up in a row. They are strewn all over the place, like they would be if we were in my room. We don't have a table for our snacks. Instead, one of the parents pulls out a bedsheet and places our food on top of it.

The L.A. Mermaids are so clearly different. We are a mishmash of faces and colors, sizes and ages. We hail from East L.A., Inglewood, Santa Monica, and Hollywood. If you compare us to the other teams, there is no question that we stand out in this pool of sameness, and this makes me happy.

I take a picture of our canopy with some of my teammates posed in front and send it to Joanne. Joanne responds with a smiley face. I can picture her in her bed, reading her manga. I wish she were here.

"Grab your yoga mats and stretch."

We follow our normal routine of stretching. Girls from other teams pause just a second too long when they pass by our canopy. I glare at them until they keep it moving. We are the only team with a boy, and that makes us extra special.

"I'm nervous," Daniel says.

"We've got to give the other teams the Look," I say.

"The look?" Daniel asks.

"Yes. The Look that we are the baddest, the best, the greatest. We are the winners." I present to them the Look. It's a combination of a serious face with a slight smirk. My look says, "Yes, I'm pretty awesome, and I know it, and you will soon know it, too."

Ayana laughs. Daniel tries to copy my face.

"Go ahead." Ayana's scowl/smile is so perfect, she kind of scares me.

"You need to do it, too." I say this to Olivia and Mayra. Regardless of how I feel about them, we're a team and we need to show a united front when it comes to dealing with our competitors.

Olivia checks with Mayra, waiting to see what she'll do. I raise my eyebrows.

"C'mon."

"Fine," Mayra says. She does the Look, and then we all do it. We're laughing so hard, we forget we're meant to be stretching, until Coach Yvette yells at us to get in the water for warm-up.

No matter how annoying Mayra and Olivia are, we are finally a team because before we dive into the water, we give the Look in unison.

After warm-ups, the judges approach their stations, where they sit with clipboards. Before we change into our sequined costumes and before the synchronized swimming dance routines, each of us will be judged individually on technical elements, like how well we can hold straight a ballet leg or whether we can do a perfect barracuda (thrust your legs vertically above the water).

I am given a number and told not to forget it. Then

I line up behind a girl wearing a black swimsuit and matching black cap. Daniel is also at my station. There's a bit of confusion while everyone tries to find their assigned stations. A woman on a microphone calls out a number, and there's yelling back and forth as someone is not where they're supposed to be.

The girl in between Daniel and me smiles and I smile back. Her face is a wall of freckles. She kind of reminds me of Princess Merida from that Disney movie.

"This is kind of cray," she says.

"Is it always like this?" I ask.

"Yeah," she says. "It always is. What team are you on?"

"L.A. Mermaids."

"We are the Aquanuts. NUTS!" she shouts, and others from her team yell back some sort of response.

Note to self: We need our very own signature call to add to the Look.

"Welcome to the chaos," she says.

We are told to get in the water. At this station, we will be judged on our crane. I have to hold my body underwater in a vertical position with one leg straight up and the other leg parallel under the surface, making like an L shape. I pray I don't mess up or forget everything Coach Yvette has taught me.

"Number fifteen."

I'm up.

Please remember everything.

I tread over to the front of the judges. Then I start to scull to flip my body backward in the water. I make sure to keep my right leg straight and my toes pointed up to the ceiling while the other leg is also pointed, but on the surface of the water. I'm doing all of this upside down, sculling and counting to ten in my head until I gently place the leg back down and flip back upright. That's it. It goes by so fast, I don't really have time to overthink things. Then we're off to the next station and the next. The scores are read out loud, but because I have to head over to the next station, I can't see what my score is. I guess I'll find out later.

After going through five stations, we're done. The girl with freckles waves goodbye and returns to her canopy while I return to mine. When I get there, everyone surrounds Coach Yvette. I know what this is. This is the moment of truth.

"Here you are." She holds up our competition swimsuit, and I can barely contain myself. It is so beautiful. There are radiant colored rhinestones on every inch of the suit. We're meant to look like the Schuyler sisters from *Hamilton,* so the swimsuit is embellished to appear to be a corset. A true costume, just like in the musical. And the headpiece! It's a dazzling crown with hundreds of rhinestones arranged like the New York skyline. Daniel's swimsuit is sequined out in blue and white to match ours. It even has a coattail.

"This is so amazing."

"Get dressed. Your group will be up soon."

We rush to the bathroom and change. My swimsuit is really snug. I guess it will stretch out in the water. And there's so much glitter, my body slowly becomes covered in it. I don't think I'll ever get rid of this glitter. I walk over to the only full-length mirror and stare at myself. I love it. I love everything about this.

There's one thing Coach Yvette forgot to mention about competing, which is that there's a whole lot of waiting around. With so many teams and age categories, there are many routines. While we wait, we land drill, making sure we remember the right counts, and then it's just a waiting game. While we wait to be called to the deck, we eat snacks, but not too many so we don't feel too full and sluggish.

"Let's go watch the other teams compete," I say. The rest of Eggbeat This! joins me, as do Mayra and Olivia.

The first team wears red outfits, and they look like walking statues. When they go on to the deck, they do so in unison. They snap their fingers, do a little hip move-ment, then get into position. Coach Yvette didn't teach us to do that. Our walk on deck is kind of boring. We'll have to work on that.

The red team dives into the water, and soon one solitary girl emerges from within. She's thrusted up into the air and does a flip, but not just any flip. Her hand is in the air in a victory pose, and she's smiling. This is all timed to the music. The crowd goes wild. After that, every single beat is a new synchronized swimming move. Cranes are not just done in slow motion here, like I just did in my figures. Nope. They do the crane super fast and add multiple kicks to it.

My jaw falls to the floor. They are so good. How can we possibly compete with that? They might be in our age group, but they are so much more advanced.

"Well, we might as well pack it up," Ayana says.

"They must be practicing their eggbeaters in their sleep," Daniel says, "their beds floating in pools for easy access."

"There's just no way," I say. The butterflies in my stomach have stopped moving and are in the same state of shock as I am.

"We can defeat them."

We all turn to Mayra, who clearly did not see the same routine. Our team doesn't come close.

"Listen to me. I've been in dance competitions since I was five years old. Every single day, I practice and practice. I know what it means to compete," Mayra says. "If you start to think you are a loser, then you will be. We're winners."

This is the first time I can actually say with conviction: Mayra is the best. I want to win. We nod in agreement with her.

"Let's go, Mermaids." Coach Yvette breaks up our pep talk.

I take a quick sip of water. Mrs. Fekadu keeps checking on our buns, adding more bobby pins to make sure our headpieces don't move. Ayana has to tell her to stop fussing. There are actual tears in Mrs. Fekadu's eyes.

"Wait a second, let me take a picture and send it to your family," Mrs. Fekadu says to me.

"Oh no, Mrs. Fekadu. Please don't send them a picture. It will just make me more nervous," I say. I'm almost sure I'm going to faint.

"Of course, I understand. No pictures," she says. And although Mrs. Fekadu agrees, I can't help wishing my parents were standing at the ready with their camera phones, waiting to document my first competition.

I stand in between Daniel and Ayana. We are ready to go. We count off and walk on deck.

"Wait for the music," I whisper.

The song begins. Mayra and Olivia dive in first. Daniel and I soon follow, with Ayana counting one beat and following us in.

In the water, there is no time to think about what the other teams have done. No time to be upset about the flip we are unable to do because it's so freaking advanced. All I can focus on is what I'm doing. How I can perfect my figures in a way so that no one will see my mistakes. I try to ignore how the new swimsuit is so tight I can barely breathe or how I have so many bobby pins stuck in my head, I'm sure my scalp is bleeding.

What I do remember to do is smile. A wide Esther Williams grin.

As we approach our grand finale, I can see Daniel is off on his counts. He's trailing and there's nothing I can do about it. All we have to do now is place our arms straight up in the air and thrust them back down for a splash. It's not a backflip or anything fancy, but it's still a nice ending. We do it, but Daniel lags a second behind. And just like that, it's over. I can't believe it. We did it! There's applause, the loudest coming from Ayana's mom, of course.

"I'm so stupid," Daniel says. He grabs his towel and walks away.

"Hey," I call to him. He ignores me. It's not his fault. I'm sure we all made mistakes.

"Well, he did mess up," Olivia says. How can the Evil Twins go from giving us a pep talk to transforming back into total jerks?

"You should talk," I say. "You were so far away from us, you looked like you were performing on your own."

"Well, you didn't even keep your legs from shaking."

Coach Yvette gets in between us. "What is going on here? Why are you all fighting? This is not how we do things. Everyone, sit down. Daniel, please, sit down."

We go to our respective mats. Daniel won't look at

anyone. As for me, I just want to pound Olivia. I was so happy, and with a snap of a finger, I'm full of rage.

"Everyone did a great job. Of course it wasn't perfect, but none of that matters. What matters is that you did it. We can only get better," Coach Yvette says. "We celebrate our accomplishments and plan for the next competition. That's it. Right now, we celebrate."

It's hard to celebrate when everyone is still so mad. We pull our phones out and continue to ignore each other. Parents urge us to eat, but I say no, which is the exact opposite of what I usually do. If my teammates aren't eating, then I won't, either. We stay like this for what seems forever, and I'm fine with that.

Then Daniel's stomach makes the loudest growling noise ever. Everyone heard it. The parents. Coach Yvette. It sounded like a monster. And within seconds, Olivia's stomach also growls, as if it were communicating with Daniel's belly. Olivia looks horrified, but her expression just makes me laugh. I can't help it. And soon Ayana laughs, too.

"Can you pass me the bag of grapes?" Daniel asks Olivia. Within seconds, we are all eating grapes and back to being a team.

The award ceremony takes a long time. There's a lot of clapping for the teams that placed. We didn't place. Not second place. Not third place. We don't even get a participation medal, which kind of burns.

The winners who placed are so happy. They pose for pictures, holding out their medals for all to see.

"I want one of those," I say.

Coach Yvette places her arm around my shoulders.

"Then there's work to be done," she says.

CHAPTER 15

"What do you think about this?" Joanne holds up a piece of silver fabric.

We are at Goodwill looking for clothing we can use to make costumes. Anime con is less than a month away and I haven't done a thing for it. I've been too busy with schoolwork and synchro practice. Lucky for me, practice was canceled today. I'm dedicating today to all things Joanne and anime con.

"I don't think the material has enough pull." We give the fabric a tug. This definitely won't work for me. "I need to be able to stretch and move."

I shake my butt to prove my point. Joanne doesn't crack a smile. She's too busy concentrating on finding the right material. Joanne has been so serious about everything. When I showed her my synchronized swimming bathing suit, hidden underneath my bed in case Mom snoops, Joanne said it looked nice. Nice? *Nice* is not what that glorious sequined eye candy is. It's brilliant, awesome, badass, amazing.

"Hey, Joanne, what do you think about this?"

I find a cowboy hat that practically swallows my head. It's only two dollars because of a hole on the brim. I can easily cover the hole with a sticker, though. Our budget for costumes is ten dollars each. It's not much because I'm still paying off my monthly team dues. My savings have slowly dwindled, and I have to find a way to make more money. Something has got to give, because at this rate I won't have any money to continue with the L.A. Mermaids. I'll definitely be kicked out.

"What would you use it for?"

"I can dress up like Cowboy Bebop, duh."

"Can you be serious?"

I still place the cowboy hat in my basket. Joanne is in a bad mood. Babysitting has taken up most of her life, while synchro has done the same with mine. When we text, it's sort of only quick responses. I realize I've been texting way more in the Eggbeat This! group.

Not today. Today I'm going to pour my attention into anime con and try not to think about money or lies or the synchronized swimming team or anything, just our friendship. But it's hard not to share the jokes and drama with Joanne. I find I'm holding back so much.

After piling our baskets with clothes and props, we head to a corner of the store to sort through the stuff.

"This isn't going to work," Joanne says. She has the biggest frown on her face.

"What are you talking about?" If she can't make sense of this mess of vintage clothing, who can? "Joanne, this is what you do! You create cool costumes from literal crap. We've done it every year for the past two years. Of *course* you can do this."

"No I can't!"

Joanne gets up, leaving behind the pile of stuff on the floor.

"Hey, Joanne, wait."

I run to her, take her hand, and walk her back. There are tears in her eyes and I try not to freak out.

"What's happening?" I say.

"I never have time for anything. There's school and homework. Then I have to rush to help take care of the baby. Cleaning him. Feeding him his bottle. Burping him. When did I become the mother? I don't know what I'm doing."

She's hyperventilating. These words have been stored in her for who knows how long. Joanne is not like me; I will virtually vomit out how I feel for everyone to hear. She's never been that type of person. I keep quiet. She needs to get the words out before they stay lodged in her throat forever.

"Also, I've realized something. I hate babies."

Oh, wow. That's not good.

"Maybe you need a break," I say. "A day when you're not thinking about diapers, like today."

We walk back to our pile. It's not fair how much re-sponsibility has been thrown at Joanne without her ever being asked. I wipe away a tear rolling down her cheek.

I feel so guilty for not being there for her. I'm a terrible friend.

"How long do you have to keep babysitting?"

"Probably till he's twenty-one years old."

We both cackle so loudly that it prompts an old lady to complain to us that we're in her way.

I think of what Dad always says when Ramón feels overwhelmed. He says to take the work one hour or even one minute at a time. If you truly love something, then you will find the space to work hard at it.

"You love anime con. Try to dedicate at least ten minutes each day to it. Every day. Dad says you have to give love to your art. Anime con is your art. Don't let the babysitting and your family take what you love away from you."

"It's easy for you to say. You're getting to do what you want."

She has a point. I am. But for me to get to do what I want, I'm pretty much lying to everyone. Plus, Ramón is about to blow my cover to my parents. The only reason he hasn't told on me is because he's been too busy with his band and practicing for upcoming Halloween parties.

"I might be doing what I want, but when my parents find out, it'll probably stop," I say. "Besides, my money is running out. I can't continue paying my dues and registration for the next competition on my own. Plus the con."

Joanne wipes the remaining tears from her cheeks. "Maybe you should stop doing it."

Why would I do that? That doesn't make sense. I've come this far. I did manage to make it through my first competition without my parents even finding out. I might as well keep going.

"No way. I plan to see this through."

I get up, a little annoyed by what she said. Is Joanne trying to sabotage me by filling me with doubt?

"We should go."

We dump the clothes we won't be using and bring the items we want to the register. Goodwill is only a couple of blocks from my house. Joanne comes over so we can finish. Meanwhile, my phone keeps blowing up. I know it's the Eggbeat This! chat. We text every single day, no exception. We even invited Mayra and Olivia to the mix, although they can be annoying. Ever since the competition, they're part of the group no matter what.

It's hard not to look at the texts, but I don't. I promised to be here for Joanne.

Joanne and I spend the rest of the day working on our costumes. My bedroom is an explosion of dirty clothes, glue guns, scissors, and a whole lot of cut fabric. I did buy the cowboy hat, and I wear it on my head while we work.

It kind of reminds me of wearing the swim cap.

"Mom has an interview tomorrow," Joanne says. She sounds hopeful.

"Where at?"

"Another factory just a few blocks away from where she used to work."

Joanne's mom has worked in some pretty tough factory jobs, the slaughterhouse being one of them. Joanne said her mother couldn't get rid of the smell when she got home. Vernon is an industrial wasteland straight from the set of *The Hunger Games*. Mom and Dad have protested in front of the factories for their illegal conditions.

"Get this. This factory insists the workers dress in white."

Dressing in white has got to be dumbest idea ever. How will they maintain a clean uniform? This also means they'll have to spend money buying multiple white outfits. The managers and owners sound like jerks.

"Who will she be working for?"

"Some fashion designer who I guess is really into the way things look."

That's not practical at all. Then it dawns on me. Why do synchronized swimmers need to have their hair gelled? How practical is that? I can do the routine just as well without having my hair cemented to my head. Why judge me on my appearance?

"We should abolish all presentation judging in

competitive sports. I mean, didn't they do away with the swimsuit portion of pageants?" This I remember because my mother made a big deal of it. She still said pageants should just be canceled altogether.

"What are you talking about?"

"I just think the owner should take into account how the workers feel about their uniforms. I bet they would work even harder if they didn't have to wear white."

Joanne furrows her brow.

"Mom can't start a protest when she doesn't even have the job yet," she says. "Besides, are you planning to tell the judges not to judge you on presentation, start a protest right at the competition?"

"Maybe."

"You sure flip-flop from loving everything about synchro to wanting to break the rules," she says.

Maybe I don't know what I'm talking about. It's like a battle is going on inside my head. I page through the fashion magazines and can tell they're classist and racist. I can see how at the competition, the judges might give the girls who look the same a better score.

No, that's not true totally true. My team sucked at our first competition. When we stop sucking, will that make a difference? It better, or I'm going full MMA on someone.

"Well, I hope your mom gets a job. Maybe then you won't have to babysit."

"Maybe," Joanne says. She lifts up the silver fabric we

nabbed at Goodwill. "I'm thinking a sash of some sort. What do you think?"

"Sounds good."

Cosplay. Fashion magazines. Synchronized swimming. Costumes to transform us into other people. I don't think that's a bad thing. I'll have to keep weighing the pros and cons in my head.

CHAPTER 16

The texts I've received from Mayra are out of control.
Each one gets more and more intense, which makes me
hesitate in responding back. It's one thing to be a member of Eggbeat This! It's quite another for me and her to
start texting each other like we're best friends. We're not.
Eventually I send back a text when I feel like it. She asks
to get on the phone.

"What's up?"

"My parents' friend is having a party and they want to
hire us to do synchronized swimming."

"How much are they paying?" Money! Exactly what
I need. Mayra tells me, and I calculate the hours and
divide it by five. "That's not enough. We would only be
getting paid like fifty dollars each if you break it down."

"No, it's only going to be me, you, and Olivia. A trio."

"Why?" We're a team, and that includes Daniel and
Ayana.

"Don't ask me. It's how they're doing it," she says.

"Anyway, do you want in, because if not I'm going to ask Ayana."

Of course I want in. It's money I can use to pay for another month's worth of dues. I had no idea I could actually turn synchronized swimming into a side hustle.

"How many times have you done this?"

"Does it matter? My mom knows a lot of people and we need a third for our trio. Are you in, yes or no? I need to tell her right away."

First, I don't appreciate anyone pressuring me to commit to anything. Second . . . There is no second. I try not to make decisions in a rush except out of anger, and I know how that usually turns out for me. I can hear Mayra's heavy breathing on the phone. I kind of like making her wait. Let her sweat it out.

"Well?"

"Mayra, I need a few minutes to think about it. I'll call you back."

I hang up right in the middle of her telling me why I need to hurry. I turn around a couple of times and do some stretches. I count to twenty and then I call.

"Okay, I'm in. Tell me the details."

After our next Saturday practice, Mayra's mom will drive us to the Palisades. The only thing I know about the Palisades is from a couple of Mom's friends. People who have a lot of money live there, and it's a place my family could never afford. Mayra confirms this by saying it's a nice house and we are not to touch a thing. She also says the only reason she invited me to do this is because we're the three best swimmers on the team.

She didn't have to tell me that. I know I'm the best.

Mom and Dad will be gone all day Saturday, and Ramón will be at band practice. Sheila is "stuck" with me, which means she can do whatever she wants while I go with Mayra. Easy.

"Okay, Mayra, I'll see you on Saturday."

This is good. I'll be making extra money by doing what I love. I can already see the possibilities. I can start advertising myself, sort of like a rent-a-magician for birthday parties, but instead it'll be rent-a-synchro-swimmer.

Mayra's mom, Mrs. Rodríguez, is really pretty. She wears a floral dress and her hair is completely straight and long, like a Kardashian. She also has long false eyelashes I can't stop staring at.

Mrs. Rodríguez works at a famous law firm on Sunset Boulevard. Mayra says she gets to meet a lot of celebrities and go to cool events, including movie premieres. No wonder Mayra can be obnoxious. She probably thinks stars are way more interesting than us, but they're not. They just have cool jobs. I also start to think about how much Mom would hate me doing this. Performing in front of rich strangers is a big no-no, but money is money and I need it.

Olivia and Mayra haven't stopped talking since we got in the car. They met in dance class when they were like five years old. Olivia was the first to stop dancing, because of a knee injury. She convinced Mayra to join her in the water.

"Thanks, girls, for the last-minute ask," Mayra's mom says. "These are big clients and I thought it would be fun to do something different."

"Thank you for asking me," I say. On my lap I hold my sequined swimsuit. The butterflies in my stomach are talking. They're not as intense as before a competition, but they're still fluttering about, confused and wondering what I'm doing. I'm venturing into the unknown with the Evil Twins. Sure, they're sorta friends of mine. Still, in the back of my mind I can't stop thinking about how Daniel and Ayana gave me questioning looks when I got in the car after practice. I told them I was doing Mayra a favor and I would tell them about it later. I've been avoiding the Eggbeat This! chat. I let Mayra and Olivia talk while I go over the routine in my head.

The house is straight out of an Esther Williams movie. I can't believe people actually live here. There are columns in front of the house. The driveway is endless and lined with rows of beautiful flowers. As for the house, it's two stories with balconies and big windows overlooking the ocean. Mrs. Rodríguez drives toward the back of the house. An older Latina greets us at the back door.

"¡Qué preciosas!" she says. "Come this way. The guests will start arriving in half an hour. You can use this room to get ready."

We walk past the kitchen, which is basically bigger than my whole house. There's a whole team of people cooking and setting up trays. An older white woman gives orders to them. She does this quietly, not in an angry voice, just very efficiently.

"You girls get ready," Mrs. Rodríguez says. "They'll let you know when to come out." Mrs. Rodríguez heads back outside to find her boss while we're set up in a large room. There's a TV, a sofa, and a tray with a whole bunch of snacks and even grown-up sparkling water to drink. I'm so nervous. I want to eat everything, but Coach Yvettte warns us not to eat too much before a competition or we might get a cramp. I hold off.

"They have the music and everything," Mayra reminds us. "We do the routine once and that's it. It's all we got to do."

"You've done this before?"

"When I was younger, Mom's boss wanted us to dance for a fundraising thing. I asked a couple of the girls from the team," she says. "It was cute. Now my mom only asks me to do it once in a while, for special events."

I wonder what's it like to perform in such a small setting. Mrs. Rodríguez said there wouldn't be too many people, a group of about twenty adults. It's strange to think they would want kids to be a part of this. It must be nice to have money, where you can ask for live entertainment. A vision of Mom staring at me disapprovingly pops into my head. I reach straight for a fancy appetizer: a cracker with cream cheese and the tiniest cucumber slice cut in the shape of a flower. For a moment, the image of Mom is gone.

Mrs. Rodríguez returns and does our makeup. It's way more elaborate than what we did at our competition. I wish she would pull off her fake eyelashes and glue them on me. They'd have to be waterproof, or synchro-proof, for me.

"Where's the pool?" I ask.

"You'll see it. It's really pretty," Mayra says. "This house used to be owned by the actor Chris Something. Right, Mom? I can't remember which Chris."

When we're done with makeup and our headpieces are set, Mrs. Rodríguez lines us up against the wall for a picture. I feel weird here with just Olivia and Mayra. It feels off, like I'm cheating on a test or something.

"I'm going to bring you out. They'll make a quick introduction, and then you do your thing," Mrs. Rodríguez says while she touches up her own makeup in the over-sized mirror.

The woman from earlier knocks on the door. The knock must be our cue. We walk out barefoot. The house is so cold, goose bumps cover my whole body. As we step outside to the backyard, guests ooh and aah. I put on the most humongous grin, which makes my jaw hurt. People are not as dressed up as I thought, but some wear cute dresses.

Mayra was right. The pool is big, not Olympic-size but almost. There's a large waterfall on one end and a separate Jacuzzi. I can even see the ocean from here.

We stand by the pool's edge. Mayra counts us off quietly as we get into position. She nods to her mother, who alerts someone to start the music.

I dive in first, with Mayra and Olivia immediately following. The water is a little too warm for my taste. We do the routine exactly as we did during our competition. Actually, we do it even better. I make sure to count to the rhythm of the music. Make sure to scull and keep my toes pointed. Make sure to give a little extra attitude whenever my head pops out of the water.

When we're done, the guests laugh and clap. They love us. I want to bottle up this feeling. In fact, I love it so much, I want to live in it. This must be how Esther Williams felt after performing.

As we pull ourselves out of the pool, we stand there wet while the guests take pictures. It's a warm fall day, but I start to tremble. Our towels are back in the room because

Mayra didn't want to ruin our looks by covering up after the routine. I'm going into shock and I can't do anything about it.

"Aren't they cute?" an older white man dressed in jeans and a button-down shirt says. He's the same man in the photos in the room we were in, pictured with important people. "Look at them."

We do our L.A. Mermaids wave, raising our hands up high and shaking them, sort of like jazz hands. Mrs. Rodríguez wants to escort us back to the room to dry off, but the man stops her.

"You guys are amazing. How long have you been doing this?"

Because this is Mayra's show, I let her answer, although everything in me wants to say something. You would think Mayra is being interviewed for television, the way she acts. It's pretty funny—and slightly ridiculous.

An older woman approaches us, dripping in jewelry. Not gold necklaces. I'm talking about big sparkly diamond rings and necklaces that probably weigh as much as baby Noah. She walks over to me with her hand outstretched. She touches my bathing suit without even asking permission. Why is she touching me like I'm a mannequin at a clothing store? My fake grin fades fast.

"I remember when I was a little girl, I used to love watching Esther Williams," she says.

"I love her!"

Finally, someone who can relate to my obsession.

"Aren't you too young to know about Esther Williams?" she says, laughing at her own joke. There are others around her who laugh at this, too.

"I've watched every one of her films," I say. "It's why I want to be a synchronized swimmer. Well, her and Anita Alvarez."

She pats my head like a dog. An actual pat.

"I didn't know synchronized swimmers could be any size."

This woman is looking right at me, though she's talking to her friends. The world stops. "Any size," she said, but she meant fat. I notice how the goose bumps on my arms intensify. I notice the looks on the faces of the people around me and I notice how I feel inside.

"Can we go now?" I say to Mrs. Rodríguez, who's busy speaking to another guest. My voice shakes just like my body.

"In a minute," she says.

They continue to sing our praises, but my stomach never lies. It's like the butterflies were warning me to abort. I look around and notice that everyone serving food to the guests is brown like me. Every single person working at this party is brown. And me? I'm this cute fat thing here entertaining these rich people. I feel so gross.

It's not the same as in the competition. When I compete, I'm competing with others. I feel equal. Here, I'm a weirdo swimmer they can point at and pet like a dog. Mayra and Olivia don't seem to mind it all, but I do. I no longer wait for Mrs. Rodríguez.

The room is empty. I wrap an oversized towel around my body and sit.

"Do you want me to bring you some food?" the woman who first greeted us asks.

"No thank you."

"Your mother must be so proud of you," she says. "Debes de ser un orgullo para ella."

I nod and try to smile, but I'm sure my smile looks more like a grimace.

When Mrs. Rodríguez, Olivia, and Mayra return, they are so happy. They ask me if I'm okay and I say yes. Later, as Mrs. Rodríguez parks in front of my house, she hands me an envelope with money. I take it. It weighs so heavily in my hand.

CHAPTER 17

Sheila is dressed up to take me to practice. She wears a miniskirt and a top that shows off her cleavage. She also wears a sparkly diamond-looking necklace. I've always loved this jewelry and even asked to borrow it, but seeing it now reminds me of last weekend and that rich woman drowning in bling. I haven't spoken to anyone about the event, not even Joanne. The money is still in the envelope, hidden underneath my bed, right by the fashion magazines.

Mom and Dad both noticed how sad I was last Saturday when I got home after the party. I told them I had an upset stomach. They seemed to believe me. I keep adding to the lies. What would my mother think if she knew I had been paid to swim for rich people? She would probably drive right up to the house, me seated in the front seat and her giving me a speech on self-respect. Then she would tell the owners off. I've seen her do this sort of thing before, but this time it would be different. This time I would have been the one who failed her. I don't like the heaviness of this shame, how it feels around my body and my heart.

"Sheila, have you ever done something you were embarrassed about?" I ask.

Sheila flips her hair back. We're waiting for the train to take us to the Expo stop.

"What do you mean? Something you swore not to do and you do it anyway?"

I nod, although it's not technically what I mean.

"Of course," she says. "I mean, have you met my mother?"

Aunt Lupe has always been strict with Sheila. Ever since the love-letter business, she's been super vigilant with Sheila. Recently Aunt Lupe made Sheila empty her pockets. She also started going over her cell phone for any evidence. Her father is always busy working, so he never interferes. It's always just Aunt Lupe being a control freak. The funny thing is I don't even think Sheila's seeing anyone. Boys are always chatting her up. My mom likes to say she has admirers. Too many to count. But I've never once noticed her pay them any real mind. She jokes with them, but it never goes past that.

"What do you do?"

"I try not to let Mom ruin every little aspect of my life. I try to find happiness," she says. A sadness sweeps across her face, and I feel bad for making her think about it. "Mom loves me. I know she does, but she's afraid. She thinks keeping me caged up will keep me safe."

There have been moments when Mom has spoken to Aunt Lupe about how she makes things worse for her daughter. Sheila's mom doesn't like to be told how to raise her kid. It's funny how Aunt Lupe and Mom both have rules on how to raise us. I'd rather have a mom who allows me the freedom to speak my mind than have someone who wants to keep me trapped. Then again, how much freedom do I really have when I'm lying to my parents?

The train arrives and my thoughts keep spinning.

Daniel and Ayana glare at me as I walk on deck. They're doing their stretches while our coaches meet. I place my yoga mat close to them, but they go from a death stare to ignoring me. I don't even get a hello.

"What's up? You forgot how to say hi?"

"Why don't you speak to your friends Mayra and Olivia?"

Now I get why they're giving me the cold shoulder. Great.

"It's not a big deal. It was just a party we performed at," I say.

"So why didn't they invite all of us, the whole team?" Ayana asks.

"I don't know. Why don't you ask them?"

Mayra and Olivia keep their heads down. For once, the Evil Twins have nothing to say.

"It's not my fault Mayra decided to invite me to that thing," I say. "Why are you punishing me for getting paid to do something?"

Daniel and Ayana look at each other.

"Think about why you were selected and why they didn't ask us."

I don't know what Daniel means by this, but I don't like it.

"What are you talking about? They asked me to do it because I'm one of the best swimmers on this team." My voice gets louder, and every time it does, the coaches look over. We're not supposed to be talking, only stretching. I don't care. "If you were my friends, you would be happy for me."

"The only reason they asked you and not us is because I'm a guy and Ayana is gorgeous. She would have stood out too much."

"Are you trying to say the only reason Mayra asked me to do it is because I'm ugly?" I want to punch someone in the face, I'm so angry.

"I didn't say anything about you being ugly. You're not at all. I think you're beautiful," Daniel says. "I'm telling you to think about why they selected you."

"Every time you talk, you're giving me ten in-and-outs," Coach Yvette warns before Daniel can explain further. "Get in the water now."

I look over to Mayra and Olivia, who have kept silent.

They have literally said nothing to prove Daniel wrong.

"Tell me the freaking truth," I say. "Why did you ask me to do the event?"

"Will you be quiet? You're going to get us in trouble," Olivia says. I get up from the yoga mat and stand over Mayra. "Tell me the truth."

"The truth is I invited you because you're the strongest swimmer on our team," she says.

"In the water," Coach Yvette yells. "Now!"

"I knew they would think it was cool to have someone who looks like you show them how it's done."

Someone who looks like me. A fat girl. A fat girl who can do twirls in the water. Mayra asked me not because I'm the best, but because I'm the fat girl who synchronize swims. Mayra and Olivia are skinny and pretty in their synchronized swimming outfits, and me? Well, I'm not like the synchronized swimmers who usually make it to the Olympics.

"You used me," I say.

"No, I didn't," Mayra says.

"Nat and Mayra, because you can't stop talking, your whole team will have to do ten more squats." Coach Yvette is losing her patience. It doesn't matter. Nothing matters.

We jump in the water. I'm fuming. We swim to the far end of the pool and pull ourselves out. Five squats before we dive back in. While we squat, I continue to mouth off.

"How dare you use me like I'm sort of experiment for your stupid rich friends."

"Nat! Stop talking. One more lap."

"Will you shut up?" This time it's Daniel who tells me to quiet down.

"Nat, I didn't use you. You are the best swimmer here. I swear."

Mayra sounds like she's about to cry. Good. I'm so mad, and I'm not sure whom I'm angrier at: Mayra for telling me the truth, Olivia for agreeing with her, or myself for saying yes to the whole thing. I swim as fast as I can across the pool, away from my so-called teammates. I wish I could swim to a whole other city.

"You guys are a bit too talkative today. Gather around," Coach Yvette says after we finish our laps. "Your next competition is in San Diego. Now, it's important that your parents attend next Saturday's meeting. We'll be going over logistics."

San Diego is too far away. I raise my hand.

"When is the competition?"

"October 30."

I didn't hear her right. It can't be. The anime con is on October 30.

"Wait, did you say October 30? I already have plans. I can't go."

"Nat, I'm not done speaking. Please stop interrupting me," Coach Yvette says firmly. "You can ask questions after I'm done."

I can't take this anymore. Everyone is out to get me. My teammates. The coach. I'm not catching a break and I refuse to accept it any longer.

"Actually, you've been mean to me all day."

Coach Yvette is totally taken aback, and so are the rest of my teammates. Ayana elbows me to stop.

"What?" Coach Yvette says, real slow-like.

"Yes, you have. You're always yelling at me. I'm not the only one on this team. Everyone's talking. Didn't you notice Mayra and Olivia? All they do is talk. Or Daniel here. Or Ayana. You're picking on me, and I don't think it's fair."

I can't stop myself. I can't control my mouth. The words just pour out.

"Nat, you can take your stuff and go. Come back when you have a better attitude."

"Fine." I pull myself out of the pool and grab everything. I walk with my head high. Coach Yvette continues to tell them about the competition. I stomp to the restroom, leaving a trail of water behind me.

Why can't they move this competition to another day? Why does it have to land on the one day I can't possibly go? The anime con is the only thing I've been saving up for. I can't miss it. Joanne wouldn't understand, and besides, I can't do that to her. I just can't. I should quit the team because honestly, who cares? Clearly my own teammates think I'm a joke.

I storm into the girls' changing room. I want to rip my stupid bathing suit off. Grab scissors and cut it into tiny pieces. I hate this. It's been forever since anyone made me feel bad about the way I look. At the rich people's house I felt shame, but I chalked it up to class. Maybe I didn't know how to act in front of people with money, but it was more than that. They saw me as a cute freak. *Look at the fat girl in the water. She's so graceful, so strong. How is that possible?*

I've been so stupid.

There is an Omar Apollo song playing in the locker room: "Invincible." Sheila was humming the song on the train ride here. Someone giggles now, and that makes me angry, too. People around me enjoying their lives while I just want to burn everything down.

I enter the cubicle to change into my clothes and stand there naked. Why was I born with this body? Why was I born to look so different than Mom or even Ramón?

No. I'm not going down that road.

"No!" I say to my reflection in the mirror. No way am I going to think this strong body is a mistake. I won't let myself fall into that hole. "I'm perfect. My body is perfect. I'm beautiful."

I grab my tote bag with my wet bathing suit and go

searching for Sheila. The slow jam still plays. I wish the music would calm me down. Instead, I want angry music, a fast-paced ranchera where I can stomp and spin in anger along with my feelings.

I round the corner where the lockers are. There is the familiar long straight hair. It's Sheila leaning into Kim. Real close. And that's when I see it. They are kissing. It's not a tiny peck like a kiss on the cheek. No, it's a full-on kiss.

It doesn't take long for them to notice me standing there, and when they do, Sheila pulls away.

"Oh, hey, Nat," Kim says. "How you doing?"

Sheila's face turns completely red.

I understand everything. The reason why Sheila happily takes me to Expo. Her being dressed up today. We are both lying to our parents because if I know anything about my aunt Lupe it's this: She would never ever accept Sheila kissing Kim.

Never.

CHAPTER 18

Sheila walks so fast, I can barely catch up. She hasn't said one word after our goodbyes to Kim. She can't even look at me, which is the weirdest feeling, to have your own cousin, the one who practically raised you, not even see you.

We pass the park and I decide to stop. Sheila has to talk to me.

"C'mon!" Sheila says.

"No, I'm not walking anymore. I'm tired of people screaming at me today. I'm sitting here."

I find a bench and wait for her to join me.

"What is it?" Sheila says when she finally sits.

"What do you mean? You and Kim."

Sheila tries to conceal the smile. Just the name Kim has her acting silly. Sheila is the cool, collected girl, the one who swats away the attention of boys. She's not cool and collected now.

"I like her. She likes me," she says. "That's all."

"I'm not . . . I mean, I don't care. I just didn't know

you're gay . . . or, wait, how do you identify?"

I live in a household where you can do and be whatever and whoever you want. Sexual orientation is not a big deal. I've attended countless marches with Mom and Dad to fight against sexism in schools and work. They even helped open an LGBTQIA+ center in Boyle Heights.

But that is not how Sheila grew up. Her parents are strict Catholics who don't believe in asking people their gender pronouns. Aunt Lupe has even made snide remarks before. When we've seen two men walking past us holding hands, she always has to joke about it. The words always hurt. There's no question: Aunt Lupe and Joe are homophobic.

"I'm gay, but you can't tell anyone," Sheila says. "It's my personal business. You understand?"

Sheila checks her phone, pulls out her lip gloss, and applies it. When she's done, she smiles at me, but it's a nervous smile.

"I understand," I say. I do, but Sheila shouldn't have to hide who she likes. It's no one's business, not even her parents'.

"I don't even know what Mom would do to me if she found out. She doesn't want anyone talking to me, let alone a girl."

I let her words sink in. How can my aunt come from the same place as my mom? They both grew up together, yet Mom is so different. She's so welcoming of everyone.

"Maybe she's changed? People change all the time."

Sheila laughs.

"The other day I was watching a television show. I forget what it was called, some show about vampires. There was a scene where two girls end up kissing. Mom asked me why I was watching something so disgusting," Sheila says. "I had to change the channel to shut her up."

Yup, that sounds about right. People don't change. Not really.

"I'm sorry, Sheila," I say. "I won't tell anyone."

"Thanks," she says. "Hey, wait a minute. Why were you done with practice so early?"

I tell her the whole story, about performing at the fancy house over the weekend and the way my teammates treated me. I also tell her about the competition.

"Today has been full of surprises," she says. "For both of us."

"I don't know how I'm going to make it to the competition and the con, but I have to," I say. "Joanne and I go every year. We never miss it."

We both sit there and think.

"You made a commitment to your team," she says. "You can't let them down."

"I think I'm going to quit," I say. "They don't like me. Even Coach Yvette was angry at me. Maybe it's not meant to be."

Sheila whips her head so fast, I'm scared she might break her neck.

"What do you mean, you're going to quit? Do you know how many hours we've spent coming back and forth to practice?" She's not yelling, but it's almost reaching that level.

"Well, we know why you've taken me to practice," I say.

"That's beside the point," she says, but it really isn't. I mean, I don't mind being used, but let's call things the way they are.

"Nat, you love synchronized swimming. You love being in the water. You love practicing the routine and you love being on a team, even if right now you don't. Don't make any decisions. Not yet. Meditate on it."

Meditate. I haven't used the app in ages because I just haven't. I don't know if it works for someone like me. Mediation and yoga are for people who walk around in overpriced yoga pants. Not this girl.

"I'll try."

Sheila drops me off.

"You're home early," Dad says when I get inside. I have to come up with a quick excuse.

"The pool ran out of chlorine," I say. Dad has a puzzled look on his face. "I know—weird, right?"

It's a terrible excuse, but it works. I lie down on my bed and turn on the meditation app. My head continues to spin. What am I going to say to Joanne? I can't let her down. Even if I'm hating on my team right now, I can't let them down, either. I meditate for ten minutes, a record for me. I don't have any solutions, but the burden doesn't seem so heavy.

"Nat, you hungry?" Without even asking, David picked up dinner for us from my favorite fast food, In-N-Out. Burgers. French fries. Even shakes. If there's anything that will put me in a better mood, it's a number-two combo with onions

"What's the word, Nat?" he asks while we eat.

"Not much."

What if I told Dad right now what's going on? How would he react? He would be disappointed, for sure, but maybe he'd also be impressed. The timing is right in that we're both basking in fast-food glory.

But I can't do it.

"So, anime con is just around the corner. Decided on what you're going as this year?" he asks.

"Almost."

"I take a sip from my milkshake. My mind is juggling so many thoughts: Sheila and Kim, the competition, my teammates, Joanne. Today was a lot. I wish I could talk things through with him.

"Dad, do you think raising boys is easier than raising a girl?"

He steals a fry from my stash and eats it before

answering. "I don't think there's an easy way. It doesn't matter if you're a boy, girl, trans, nonbinary. . . . Growing up is hard, and we—meaning us parents—make mistakes. I make mistakes." Dad scrunches up his face. "What's on your mind, Nat?"

"Nothing. Just wondering," I say. "I better start on my costume. Joanne is coming over tomorrow." We finish our meal, but Dad lingers a bit by my bedroom door, checking on me. I think he feels like I want to share something with him, but I can't. I need to figure this whole thing out myself.

Joanne models her costume. This year she's going as Mikasa Ackerman from *Attack on Titan*. Mikasa is a pretty badass character, with a green cape and cool swords. Joanne has made her swords from stiff cardboard. Because her parents are not fans of any of this, she usually keeps her cosplay stuff at my house. I'm dressing like Maka Albarn from *Soul Eater*. Maka wears a pretty simple duster, with boots and a long scythe. Both of our outfits are practically done. I just need to finish painting the cardboard scythe.

"I can't wait," Joanne says. She's been studying video tutorials on how to get Mikasa's makeup just right. The more she raves about the con, the more my anxiety increases. I don't know how I'm going to break the news.

"Why aren't you getting dressed?" she says.

I reluctantly put my Maka costume on. I look great. Then why can't I get into it mentally? I have to tell her.

"So, what happens if I can't make it to the con?" I say this real quick. Joanne's face collapses into a ball of confusion.

"What do you mean?"

I play with my oversized scythe. It took us hours to get it right. This is so hard.

"I guess what I mean is that I have a competition in San Diego on the same day of the con."

Joanne looks down at her costume and slowly starts to take it off. She doesn't say a word. This makes me feel so much worse. I start to talk real fast.

"I didn't know they were going to have a competition. Also, it's in San Diego, and who knows how I'll make it there, but I should go. Right? I mean, I've been paying the monthly dues. We're a team. . . ."

Joanne continues to peel off the costume. She folds it neatly on the bed. I know this face so well. She's about to cry, and the lump in my throat grows.

"It's not like we haven't been planning this for months," she says quietly.

"I mean, maybe I can't even go. Listen. It's not like I have a ride to San Diego, so I'm probably worrying for nothing."

Joanne gets up.

"Ever since you joined the Mermaids, you haven't had

any time for me. We barely talk and when we do, you usually only talk about synchronized swimming," she says. Her voice shakes a bit. "And that's fine. Just don't promise to do something and not do it."

"That's not true. We wouldn't have made these costumes if I had ignored you," I say. I've juggled all kinds of things ever since I joined the team. I deserve a little credit. "I'm doing my best."

"The best for the team, for your new friends."

"Joanne, I told you I might not even be able to make it, so this is just a big fat maybe."

Joanne no longer looks at me.

"I'll quit the team. It's no big deal. I can't keep lying to my parents, and there's no way they'll let me go to San Diego, especially since they have no clue what I'm doing."

"Don't."

I don't understand. Isn't that what she wants me to do? I would never want to hurt her in any way. Can't Joanne see that? If being on the team is causing her this much pain, then it's not worth it.

"Don't quit the team. That's not fair of you to lay that on me."

Joanne heads to the door. I grab her arm.

"Wait. If I want to quit the team, I will. You can't tell me what to do."

"No! You don't get to act out because you feel sorry for me. Do what you want to do. Leave me alone."

Before I can even respond, Joanne walks out the house, almost knocking down my brother in the process.

"Whoa, what's going on?" Ramón says to Joanne. She keeps walking. "Are you fighting?"

There's nothing I can do to stop Joanne from leaving. Nothing I can do to get rid of these feelings I have. I close the door behind her and take off my costume.

CHAPTER 19

For whatever reason, the pool is not heated for today's practice. Each time we complete the routine, we have to step out of the pool. The goose bumps on my legs are out of control. It's hard to stay in starting position when your whole body is trembling.

"Again," Coach Yvette says.

At first I was totally into listening to the *Hamilton* soundtrack. I thought it was cool to create a synchronized swimming routine to the music, with Daniel being Hamilton. Fun idea. Well, after listening to the damn song more than five million times, it makes you want to kill someone. I really and truly can't stand *Hamilton*—and I never thought I would say that.

"I hate this routine," Daniel says.

There's a part when the girls have to lift him up. Everything above water must look graceful and perfect. Below the surface, limbs and arms scramble to do the next move. It can get really ugly down there.

"Will you stop kicking my stomach," Mayra says to me in more of a growl than an ask.

Okay, maybe the last kick was totally unnecessary. Am I still angry over what she said to me last practice? Yes. If anything, I'm really good at holding grudges.

When I returned to practice, Coach Yvette took me aside and we went over my "incident" from last week.

"If you don't want to be here, you don't have to come," she said. "It's not to say we don't love having you here, but I don't tolerate disruptions during practice. If you're dealing with something, you can come speak to me privately."

She said I could talk to her about anything. Then this weird thing happened: I actually told her about my fight with Joanne. I don't know why. It just came out.

"She thinks I'm abandoning her because I'm here," I said. "I feel really bad."

"I'm so sorry. It's happened to me when I first joined a team. It's hard to find the right balance with this and schoolwork and friends," she said. "This is new for you. Don't be so hard on yourself. You'll make time for your friends. Just think of a way you can make it up to her."

It's hard to make it up to a person when they're no longer answering your texts. All I can do is keep trying, I guess. At least Coach Yvette was really understanding about everything. She's pretty cool, but right now she's relentless.

"I know you're tired, but let's do it again and then you can go," Coach Yvette says.

We go through the routine once more. I recite the counts in my head, but I can barely lift my arms anymore. I don't kick Olivia or Mayra, but I think it's because I've run out of energy. We all have. The routine is so blah, even Coach Yvette can't muster much praise.

"Okay, hit the showers and don't forget, permission slips are due today, so if you haven't handed them in already, do not leave without doing so."

Thankfully, my permission slip signature was forged by Sheila already. I walk past her and wave hello to Kim. I need to start setting the pieces down for my ridiculous new plan.

Last night, I figured it all out. The con is this weekend. Our competition in San Diego is set for early in the morning. We should be done by 2:00 p.m. If we drive right back to Los Angeles, I can still make it to the con by 4:00 p.m. That gives Joanne and me a couple of hours together. Joanne would be happy. I would be happy. It's a win-win.

"So, Ayana. How are you getting to San Diego?" I ask. "Are you driving?"

"How else?" she says, slightly annoyed. "I can't teleport there. Can I?"

"Hahaha. Good one," I say, although I know I sound fake. Ayana eyes me with distrust, as she should.

"Think I can hitch a ride with you?"

Easy enough ask.

"We're already taking Emily."

Emily is on the intermediate team. She's really sweet, always asking us if we need help with our figures. I like her. Her mom usually brings her to practice. I don't understand what makes the San Diego competition any different.

"Why can't her mom take her?"

"Not that it's any of your business, but her mom is undocumented and she doesn't feel safe driving to San Diego," Ayana says. "She asked if we could take her a while back."

I understand. The drive south would be too much of a risk for her family. Here I am trying to pull a fast one while Emily and her family deal with real issues.

I think about the choices I'm making, how I'm willing to deny my own parents this special event while Emily doesn't have a choice.

"That sucks."

"Yeah, it does. Sorry, Nat. I would squeeze you in the car, but my mom doesn't handle change well."

I can't ride with Olivia and Mayra, either. There's no room in the minivan with their families. I'm running out of options. "Thanks anyway, Ayana."

I wait outside while Sheila says goodbye to Kim. Their time together is limited, so I give them privacy. Besides, I need to think.

Daniel stands by himself, waiting to be picked up. I didn't think about asking him. I guess I thought he would say no. There's no reason for this. I have nothing to lose.

"Hey, Daniel," I say. "Are you going to San Diego?"

"Yeah. Aren't you?"

"I don't have a ride yet. Do you think I can go with you?"

He rubs his forehead. If Daniel says no, then I'm not sure what I'll do. I guess I can take a train, but I doubt there would be one leaving early enough. Coaches aren't allowed to drive us to competitions—something having to do with it being a liability.

"I'll have to ask," Daniel says. "I guess it should be okay."

The way he says this makes me wonder if he's still upset with me. It's not like anything was resolved. My problem with Joanne kind of overtook the incident. One fire at a time, I guess, or at least that's what Dad taught me. I'm really trying to hold everything together: my friendship with Joanne, my place on this team, and Sheila's lie. I'm juggling as fast as I can.

"Well, if it's too much of an ordeal, don't worry about it."

I've never been shy about asking people for things. I don't really care what they think, but ever since the fancy house I find myself doubting everyone and everything.

Like, are they being nice to me because they like me, or are they faking it? Does Daniel feel sorry for me—and why am I getting angry about this?

"It's not an ordeal. I said I have to ask my mom. I don't know how you can ask me for a favor and be mad at my answer." Daniel shakes his head.

I need to apologize. I keep steamrolling through everyone, and I have to stop.

"I'm sorry. I'm being rude," I say. "I appreciate you asking. Thank you."

I start to walk back to the entrance, ready to text Sheila to hurry up. Seconds later, Daniel's mom appears. He leans in through the car window. I watch him ask his mother. She looks over to me. I stand up straight and tuck my hair away from my face. I don't know why I do this.

Daniel jogs over.

"Mom says yes but she wants to talk to your mom, just to confirm. You're still pretending?" Again with my mom.

"Yeah."

Daniel shrugs. I take down the number.

"I'll make sure to have her call," I say, although I don't know how. At least I have a ride to San Diego. That's what counts. First part of my plan is in place. Now for the second part.

✦ ✦ ✦

Our dinner table is covered with postcards. Mom has enlisted a few of her students and friends to join her in a postcard-writing campaign to congressmembers regarding immigration laws. There's an impromptu potluck situation happening.

"¡Hola, Sheila! Baby girl!" Mom says. "Grab a plate and take a seat."

"I should be heading home," Sheila says. Sheila gets weird around Mom. I think she finds her intimidating.

"Nonsense! Go eat. There's plenty of food."

Sheila reluctantly makes herself a plate and so do I. The majority of people here are women—just a couple of male students. The students are in the living room, and Ramón is with them. He likes to talk to them about college life. I sit by Mom.

"After you finish eating, we want everyone to contribute at least five postcards," she says.

Sheila raises her eyebrows. She doesn't like to be part of anything political, but Mom won't take no for an answer.

Neither will I.

"Hey, Mom, there's this school thing happening next Saturday. It's a morning thing, and I'm meeting Joanne at the con afterward. They promised to drop me off."

Sheila doesn't want to be in the same room while I devise my latest ridiculous lie, but she stays. I promised her it would be my last. It has to be.

Everyone around the table laughs at a story being told

by my mother's coworker. I don't get it, but the timing is exactly right for asking for favors. Mom can barely contain herself. She's cracking up. I might as well drop my little bomb.

"Is it okay if you call Daniel's mom? They're going to give me a ride to the school thing."

I start to dial the number to Daniel's mom. It's hard for Mom to concentrate when the jokes keep getting worse. Sheila stares at me with her mouth open.

"Mom, please let her know you're okay with me going with them."

Daniel's mom answers the phone, and although my house is so loud with laughter, I keep going with the plan.

"Hi, this is Nat. I have my mom here. Do you want to speak with her?"

I hand the phone over to Mom, who looks at it with such confusion. She grabs it in between cackles.

"Yes, hi! So nice to meet you."

My heart is in my throat. All she has to do is say yes.

"Mom, say yes. Please just say yes."

Mom covers the mouthpiece and tells me to be quiet. "Of course. Thank you so much for taking her. I'm sure she'll have fun."

Because I need to get her off the phone before she asks for more details, I spill a glass of water on the postcards. Everyone gasps and runs to help save them.

"Nat!" Mom yells. She apologizes to Daniel's mom. I

take the phone from her and thank Daniel's mom again.

"Sorry."

I grab paper towels and vow to rewrite every single one of the postcards. Another person tells a joke and Mom is back at it. I'm good to go. I grab a bunch of the postcards and start writing. I even hand a few to Sheila.

"That was terrible," Sheila whispers, knowing full well the amount of acting I just did to make this weekend's trip a possibility.

"It worked, though," I say triumphantly.

"Sure, but for how long?"

Mom looks so happy surrounded by her friends.

"Not long. I promise I'll stop with the lies soon. I swear."

CHAPTER 20

Daniel's parents are eager to hit the road. In the back seat, I notice a tiny head slumped against the window.

"Don't worry, she won't wake up," Daniel says.

Daniel's sister Gina is five years old. She wears glasses and is one of Daniel's biggest fans. At practice, she takes it upon herself to hold his towels out for him, like she's his very own assistant. I sit in the middle and try not to disturb her sleep.

Daniel concentrates on finishing his bowl of instant oatmeal. His mother offers me a bowl as well and I take it. Daniel hasn't really looked at me, and I can't help but wonder if he's annoyed that I'm here. Maybe he's just not a morning person.

"Thank you for the ride," I say.

"Of course, glad we can help," Daniel's mom says.

San Diego is about two hours away, which should get us to the competition a little before 8:00 a.m. This early-morning situation is murder. I eat the oatmeal and I'm so grateful. I snuggle into my hoodie. Daniel is already nodding off and we haven't even left Los Angeles yet. I'm sleepy, too, but it's hard to sleep when you have so many things racing through your head.

It took everything in me to be able to convince Joanne that I would meet her at the con at 4:00 p.m., dressed and ready to go. After ignoring my texts for a couple of days, she finally responded. We met up at her house, where I did a whole lot of begging. She wanted to cancel our plans, but we can still make this happen. All I have to do is make sure I leave San Diego by 2:00 p.m. No problem.

"See you later!" I text Joanne, although she's probably still sleeping. This has to work.

"How did you get into synchronized swimming?" Daniel's mom, Mrs. Johnson, asks.

"I saw the Mermaids perform and I liked it," I say.

"Daniel must have told you how his older sister was a synchronized swimmer," she says. "Daniel would follow her around the pool just like that little sleepyhead there. They love the water."

Daniel seems embarrassed. I think it's sweet. I used to follow my older brothers around, too.

"Lety thought I was annoying," he says.

"She did? Oh well, that's what happens when you have a big family," Mr. Johnson says. Daniel looks a lot like his father. Tall and lanky.

"I'm just glad we found a team that's progressive," Mrs. Johnson says. "Not all teams were welcoming. Instead of saying they didn't want him, they kept saying they couldn't accommodate him."

"Well, he's on a good team now. It's all that matters," Mr. Johnson says. "Sports should be willing to be coed. Don't you think?"

Daniel's parents are a bit like mine. Daniel's father works as a chiropractor, while his mother owns a day care. They're much older than my parents.

"Yes, I think all sports should be coed," I say. "Everyone should have a chance to be a part of a team."

It must have been hard for Daniel to try out so often and then be turned away. We both lucked out when we found the L.A. Mermaids. I turn to tell Daniel this, but his eyes are closed. I guess I was hoping we would talk a bit. Oh well.

Daniel's parents have classical music on. It's so soothing. Soon my eyes feel heavy and I give in to the quiet. Hopefully when I wake up, we will be in San Diego.

The honk from a car startles me awake. I don't remember when I fell asleep on Daniel's shoulder, but there it is. I think I may have even drooled.

"Sorry," I say.

Daniel rubs his shoulder as if my big head left a dent.

"Where are we?" he asks.

"We're about fifteen minutes away," his father says. "Almost there. Anybody want snacks?"

They've changed the music from classical to R&B. I like to call this old-people music. Daniel's mom hands bags of dried fruits and water bottles to both of us. Funny, his sister hasn't moved yet. I can't help but notice that Daniel still hasn't made eye contact with me. There's this weird uncomfortable thing going on between us and I don't like it.

"Daniel, are you angry with me or something?" I whisper so his parents and his still-sleeping sister can't hear.

"No, not really."

Not really? He *is* angry.

"You're mad at me for that whole thing with Mayra and Olivia. It's not fair. They invited me. It wasn't the other way around."

"You should take responsibility for your actions," he says.

This is the moment when I would honestly tell him the many ways I think he's wrong, but I'm in his parents' car and I keep thinking of the meditation app. So I breathe in and breathe out. I slowly count to ten before responding.

"I did it because I wanted to make money, but now I'm just embarrassed by the whole thing. Saying yes, going, and the way I acted afterward. I don't even want to think about it," I say. "Later today I'm going to spend the money I made on something silly to help me forget."

We go quiet as his parents argue about where they

should park the car. At least I didn't attack Daniel, and that feels different. I'm so used to arguing with people because they don't see my point of view. This is new for me.

"Want some more?" he asks, opening another bag of dried mango strips. I nod and smile.

We look out the window. There are so many girls in their uniforms. They look so ready, so prepared. I'm still wearing my oversized sweatpants and hoodie.

"I'm getting nervous," Daniel says.

"So am I," I say.

"You? You never seem nervous about anything," he says.

"My parents always tell me I'm the best," I say. "It's not my fault I believe them."

" 'I'm the best.' Is that how you do it?"

"Yeah," I say. "You repeat it until you believe it's true."

Knowing Daniel is nervous only makes me want to act braver than I feel.

Gina finally wakes up and she has so much energy, it's impossible for her to sit still. I don't blame her—I feel the same way. When we finally park the car, we practically jump out.

Daniel's father grabs Gina's hand. "Ready to go and do some exploring?" Mr. Johnson and Gina walk away while Daniel and I grab our backpacks and head through the facility toward the outdoor pool.

Compared to the Expo Park pool, the swimming facility here looks brand-new. Fancy pool deck with outdoor showers and a cool waterslide. Most of the other competitors are set up by the pool, and they, too, look new: New beautiful team uniforms. New banners. Even the parents are wearing matching team T-shirts.

When we find the L.A. Mermaids team spot, there's no bright banner stating who we are. Instead, there's the raggedy canopy that has seen better days. And we're still such a mishmash of girls. Big. Small. Girls with smiles, happy to start the day. Others with mean faces looking like they wished they had stayed home, like Ayana, whose mother is asking her to zip up her parka. It is chilly, and if Ayana doesn't want to wear her parka, I sure wouldn't mind it. Parkas are expensive. Maybe next year I'll buy one—if there's a next year for me.

"Good morning!" I say this loudly because why not? Ayana glares. Mayra and Olivia mumble a hello, and Daniel behind me chuckles.

"We're going to kick some *bootay* today! I can feel it."

Ayana moans at my display. "Please don't. It's too early in the morning for all that."

Before I start singing the *Hamilton* song to really annoy Ayana, Coach Yvette appears, clutching a coffee like it's going to save her life.

"Okay, Mermaids," she says. "You know what to do."

Everyone pulls out their yoga mats and stretches. This competition doesn't test our figures, only the dance routines. We spend a couple of hours stretching on the deck until it's our turn to warm up in the water and go over our routine. I try my best to concentrate. There's a large clock on the building. I need everything to go as smoothly as possible. I can still meet Joanne. The schedule must stick. Once practice is done, we wait under our canopy, land drilling until the competition begins.

Routines are divided by age groups. I love watching the tiny young swimmers. They are so cute. The parents form a wall to try to capture the magic with their cell phones. Soon enough, it's time to get ready. I give Daniel a high five and head to the restrooms. The place is bustling with action. Mothers are heating up water in portable teakettles to use for gelling hair. Others are applying makeup. Lucky for me, Ayana's mother quickly gels my hair. Then she runs out to touch up our other teammates before we find a corner and start stripping. There are no stalls available, so we huddle close together and get undressed. You can't really get hung up on what you look like, not when you have to quickly get ready.

Another group of swimmers joins us. They must be in our age group. They have really nice uniforms. I smile at them, and they smile back. Even if we're supposed to be sworn enemies, there's no reason not to be nice.

"Hey, did you notice there's a boy swimming this year?" a swimmer with almost white-blonde hair asks, and I know where this is going. Ayana shakes her head at me, a warning not to say anything.

"We've got to hurry," Ayana says. I try to ignore the girls talking.

"There's no other guy doing synchronized swimming. I mean, can't we just have one thing for us?" Blonde Hair says this like we should be in agreement, and I want to punch her in the face. Who is she to turn her horrible opinion into a feminist rally?

"I'm sorry, who are you?" I inch closer to her. Olivia places a hand on my shoulder. I know I should stop, but I can't because this anger is rising. "What makes you think we want to know your opinion on who gets to be a synchronized swimmer?"

Teams are being announced through a loudspeaker. We need to go, but all I can think is how much I need to school this girl in front of me. Others in the locker room look a little scared. I don't care. I want her to explain herself.

"I don't think boys should be on synchronized swimming teams," she says. Just like that, like her words are final.

"Yeah, well, I don't think mean girls with no sense should talk when no one here asked."

"I can say whatever I want."

"It's not worth it, Nat. Let's go," Mayra tries to intervene. "They're calling us."

But there's no turning back. I'm going in.

"There are repercussions for saying things out loud."

"Oh yeah? Like what?"

"Let's square up," I say.

"Square up?" she laughs. "Are you part of a gang or something?"

That's it. I'm about to show her what type of gang I'm a part of.

"Don't do it," Ayana says. Mayra and Olivia keep me from grabbing the girl's face and showing her what's what.

"L.A. Mermaids! What are you doing?"

Coach Yvette is livid. She leads us out of the bathroom. We stomp our way to the deck as the team before us gets into position. Daniel waits with a confused face.

"How dare you jeopardize today by engaging in such terrible behavior," Coach Yvette whispers. I raise my hand to say something and the face she gives me in return is the same one my mother has given me. "Do you understand we're the only team here with a diverse group of swimmers? Do you know what that means? Most people can't wait for us to fail. And here you are, playing right into the stereotypes they expect from us."

"I'm not a stereotype." I say this quiet-like, but I know she heard it. "I was defending my teammates."

"Defend them in the water," she says. "Prove to them you're way better than they are in the sport they think you do not belong in."

"But sometimes that's not enough. You have to tell—"

"And sometimes it doesn't matter what people say or think about you. Your actions affect everyone on your team," Coach Yvette interrupts me. "Think of that before you react."

Pause. I didn't pause. It's what Ramón tells me to do. What Sheila and my parents have said. I've made a mistake. Again. All I can do is stare at my toes.

"I'm so disappointed in all of you. You are to check each other outside the water, just like you do in the water."

"L.A. Mermaids, get to your positions."

There is no time to wish each other luck. No time to weigh in on what Coach Yvette says. It's hard to think of the routine when the lump in my throat is growing by the second. I take a deep breath in, and it catches, and I know I'm going to do what I almost never do: I'm going to cry. I adjust my goggles to let a tear slide down, and that just makes things worse. I can't stop crying.

But the music begins.

We start our routine and it's impossible for me to re-member the counts or what I'm supposed to do next. I'm not the only one messing up. Mayra and Olivia make mistakes, too. Daniel is the only one on time, but he can't carry the team. We suck and it's my fault. Soon the song is over, and so is our routine. Parents pity-clap for one of the worst performances ever.

No one says a word after we get out of the pool. Everyone is angry or sad at our performance. The parents try to cheer us up, but it's not possible. I brush away my tears and force myself to stop crying. Then I stare at my phone and watch the time slowly tick away. Medals will be given out soon. We'll have to sit there and clap while everyone else around us wins. I feel like crap.

"We're leaving right after the ceremony," Daniel's mom reminds me. They want to avoid traffic. I can still make it to the con. I should be happy, but instead I'm miserable.

"Can you tell them to find another freeway to take?"

Daniel looks at me like I'm being ridiculous. We're in bumper-to-bumper traffic, still at least an hour away from reaching Joanne.

"How? I don't know if you've noticed, but this car doesn't levitate."

Daniel is annoyed. I'm annoyed, too. I'm trying hard not to freak out. We left with more than enough time to make it the con. More than enough. And yet here we are in this hell pit filled with nonmoving cars, and there's nothing I can do about it.

"Almost there," I text Joanne again. She stopped responding after the fourth text.

When we finally reach the con venue, I practically scream, "Just drop me off right here."

I jump out and walk around. I can see Joanne. There are still hundreds of people milling around in their costumes. We can do this.

"Joanne!"

She has a long face and I know she's angry. It's okay. I made it. I still kept my promise!

"Let's go. C'mon!" I speedwalk toward the entrance.

"There's no point. It's over."

"What do you mean it's over? We can still do it. It's just a little after five-thirty. It's not a lot of time, but we can still get through—"

"No. Everything is closed. They closed at five."

"What?"

"Yes. You're late. You said you would be here by four. It's almost six. I've been waiting here since three-thirty. I'm going home."

Joanne takes the two long swords and throws them in the garbage.

My heart drops.

CHAPTER 21

As I approach my house, I notice my aunt's car in the driveway and I wonder if this day can get any worse. Daniel's parents were kind enough to drive me home after they made sure Joanne got on the right bus. They wanted to squeeze her into the car, but she refused. The drive was more than enough time to contemplate how she's never going to speak to me again.

"Thank you," I say to them before they drive away, and I cautiously enter my house.

I should have known better. I should have asked Daniel's family to adopt me right then and there.

"Where is Sheila?" my aunt Lupe screams the minute I open the front door.

"I don't know," I say.

Her hair is frazzled. My whole family is in the living room. I can tell from their serious faces that this has been going on for some time.

"She said she was with you," Aunt Lupe says.

And now I'm forced to think about whether I'm

meant to cover for Sheila, although she didn't ask me to. I have no idea what's going on. Did she use my trip to San Diego for a date with Kim? Why wouldn't she tell me?

Mom gives me a look, one that says I'd better fess up to whatever mess I'm in.

"Where have you been?" Mom says.

"I told you. I was with Daniel and his family for this school thing and then I went to the con."

"What is going on with your hair?" Mom comes over to me and tries to run her hand through my hair. It is completely immovable from the gel. I thought I could sneak into the house and take a quick shower to remove it. Ramón shakes his head. The gel is the least of my worries.

"What's going on?" Dad asks. He's also upset with me. I don't have any schemes or words to get myself out of this hole I've made.

There's a knock at the door just then. Aunt Lupe runs to answer it like she lives here. She is so angry. I know who's going to be behind it, and I'm afraid for her because Aunt Lupe is full of rage.

"Tell me right now where you have been all day, because you weren't with Natalia!" Sheila hasn't even fully entered the house; her mother blocks the way.

"Will you close the door?" Mom says. "We don't need to alert everyone about our business."

"I was out," Sheila says. This is probably not the best approach right now, but she's sticking to it. As for me, I'm trying my best to avoid the onslaught about to rain down on her and on me.

"Where were you? With that boy?"

My aunt digs through her purse and then holds sheets of paper in her hand. Are those printouts of Sheila's emails? Oh no.

"Who is this?"

"You read my emails?" Sheila says. She can't even scream about it.

"Lupe, por favor. Don't do this," Mom implores. "You should have never gone through her personal stuff."

"No! No! There's no such thing as personal when she's a minor living under my roof. I'm not like you, who lets their kids roam free without any supervision."

"That's not fair or true," Dad says.

"Where have you been?" Aunt Lupe screams. Her face is red and her eyes are bulging. Because I'm no fool, I start slowly walking to my bedroom.

"Nat." Mom stops me. "What's been going on? What have you been doing?"

"Nothing. I've been . . ."

"Enough with the lies. Tell me right now where Sheila has been taking you."

I look over to Sheila. There's no point. She's drowning in her own problems.

"Sheila has been taking me to synchronized swimming practice."

"Excuse me?"

Ramón sits down. Everyone is caught in this.

"I joined the L.A. Mermaids."

"Wait one second. Did we not say no to you joining the team? Weren't we clear?" Mom is angry, although she's trying to stay calm. "You've been lying to us all this time?"

"I knew you didn't want me to," I say.

"And so you decided the best course to take was to lie to your parents and have Sheila take you to practice. I am speechless."

"What else have you been lying about?" Sheila's mother asks.

"I'm tired of explaining my whereabouts," Shelia says. "All I do is take care of Nat. You're constantly breathing down my neck every five minutes. I can't stand it."

"Who is this?" Aunt Lupe shoves the papers in front of Sheila's face.

Sheila grabs the papers and rips them up.

"Her name is Kim," she says.

The thoughts going through Aunt Lupe's mind are so intense, I want to take cover.

"Please sit down and let's talk this over," Mom begs.

Aunt Lupe is not interested, not at all. "No. I want you to go home and pack all your stuff. You think you know what you're doing? Then you can figure this life out by yourself."

"What? You can't be serious," Sheila says. She starts to cry, and I feel my tears coming, too.

"Don't do this," Mom says.

"No! I'm done. She's going out with a girl," Aunt Lupe says. "As if there aren't enough problems in this world, she has to play around with girls."

"What kind of homophobic statement is that?" Mom says.

"Of course you would side with her. You think everything is perfect because you are so open and so free," Aunt Lupe says. "Look at your own children. Look at Nat. She's so free that she's lying and dragging Sheila with her."

This is definitely my fault. If I hadn't been kicked out of Roosevelt Pool, I would have never made it to Expo Park pool, would have never taken the challenge to be on the team. I'm the bad seed. The one who always messes up.

"Everyone is upset," Dad says. "Let's just sit down and talk."

Aunt Lupe huffs. "You people think conversations are easy. I do everything right and I still end up with a no-good daughter who would rather fool around than fly straight."

"I'm a good person," Sheila sobs. I feel her words in my heart. Ramón walks over to Sheila to console her.

"Don't bother coming to the house," her mother says. "I'm through."

Aunt Lupe grabs her purse and storms out, slamming the door behind her. Sheila cries so hard, she can hardly breathe. Ramón walks her to the kitchen, urging her to drink water.

"Why, Nat?" Mom asks. "I feel like we're always open with you, with both you and your brothers."

It's my turn. I'm so tired. I've been taught to always be truthful, but only to a certain extent. I'm vocal for the rights of others and when I want to get my way, but now, when I have my mother imploring me to be honest, I want to be quiet. But I can't keep this in, even if it hurts.

"The truth is, you don't let me have my own beliefs," I whisper, barely getting the words out. "I have to believe what you believe."

"That's not true. We always have discussions about everything."

Dad sits with Mom on the sofa. I'm the only one standing, and this is exactly how it feels—I'm forced to plead my case to two of the smartest people alive. They live for arguing, for proving everyone else wrong. It's hard to find your voice when this is what your parents do and they're so good at it.

"No, Mom. There's only your opinion. You said synchronized swimming is just a pageant on the water and it glorifies beauty over hard work. How am I supposed to argue with that? I like synchronized swimming. I like the costumes. I like the sequins. I feel pretty and strong when I do it."

"You are pretty and strong. You don't need a costume to make you feel that way."

I look at her. It's so easy for her to say those things. Sometimes when we walk together, I feel people look at her and wonder what went wrong. Like, what gene skipped me? She doesn't see what I do, or maybe she chooses to ignore it.

"I don't *feel* that way all the time. Just because you say it to me doesn't make it true," I say.

Mom doesn't know what to say. She wants to argue because that's what we do. We find ways out of situations with smarts, but sometimes there is no right answer, no easy solution. Sometimes there is only hurt.

"I'm sorry. I only want the best for you and to provide you with the tools for you to win in this life," she says. "It didn't mean lying your way through life, lying to us."

"If we say no to you, then we probably have a valid reason for doing so," Dad says.

"You say you want me to learn how to make my own decisions. You also tell me you want me to fight for the things I believe in. I did," I say, my voice breaking. "I can't even look at fashion magazines because you hate them. I know the models don't represent ideal beauty. I know synchronized swimmers are mostly thin and white and look all the same, but I wanted to prove I can do it. That I can be beautiful and graceful in the water. Me."

I don't know if there's anything more I can say. I feel empty. I can't take standing here while my parents decide where they went wrong with me.

"Can I go now?"

After a few beats of silence, Mom and Dad nod. I get in the shower to finally take the gel off. I can still hear Sheila crying. I'm crying, too.

CHAPTER 22

It's Sunday, and Sundays are meant for the family to get together and catch up from the week, but this week has been full of so much drama. Even from bed, I can hear my dad clanging around the pots and pans. He's probably making us breakfast—pancakes, scrambled eggs, and muffins, with mimosas for Mom. He has Bad Bunny playing to try to lighten the mood. I'm not sure it's going to work.

I feel Sheila stir next to me as she grabs another tissue from the box. Sheila's been crying all week. My aunt refuses to allow her back home—not even after my mother went over to their house late last night to try to talk things through. I heard Mom say that Sheila's father didn't say a thing about the matter. Whatever Aunt Lupe says is final, I guess, but it's hard to believe.

"Are you hungry?" I ask.

"No."

For the past week, Sheila has slept in my room.

There have been many periods when Mom has let a

young person stay with us while they work out their next move. Kids whose parents refuse to accept them for who they are. I just never thought that would happen to my own cousin.

My stomach growls. Unlike Sheila, I'm starving, and although I'm still sad about everything, I will eat because food is vital and I refuse to let that go. I leave Sheila and head to the kitchen.

"Good morning, Nat. How did you sleep?"

Dad tries to be in a good mood. It hasn't been easy for anyone in this house.

This week I stopped going to synchronized swimming practice. I had to call Coach Yvette and Coach Renée to explain why I wouldn't be returning. They were definitely surprised that I'd lied to my parents and to them. I apologized, and now I have to make up for everything I did to the team and to my parents. I'm not sure exactly how. My parents haven't clued me in yet on this part of my punishment.

"I slept okay."

Mom is still in her room. We haven't really been talking to each other. I don't know what to say to her. I don't think she knows what to say to me. This has never happened to us before.

"Good morning." Ramón enters with his hair out of whack. "Where's Sheila?"

I nod to the bedroom and Ramón shakes his head.

He's been extra nice to our cousin, to both of us, really, although he also got in trouble for keeping our secrets. Everyone is punished.

In school I walk around in a daze while classmates keep asking me if I'm sick. They don't know how to react to me, especially when I'm not really talking or arguing or scheming like usual. They also keep asking why I'm not hanging out with Joanne. When they do, my heart feels so heavy. It's like I'm walking around with a dark cloud pressing down on my head.

The Eggbeat This! group chat was a steady stream of questions about why I was missing practice. I miss it so much. Still, it bums me out to read their complaints about Coach Yvette making them do in-and-out squats. So I've decided not to go on there anymore.

Dad puts a plate of my favorites (pancake and bacon) in front of me. Mom will join us soon and I wonder how this family get-together will play out.

"Do you think I should save some for Sheila?" Dad asks.

"Yes, we probably should," I say.

The other night in bed I said sorry to Sheila for the trouble I got her into. She said I didn't need to apologize, because what happened with her mom was bound to happen. Also, she did what she did because she wanted to. Sheila gave me a big hug and then she got teary. I ended up showing her videos of funny synchronized swimming faces. Synchro Face is what I like to call them. It made her laugh.

"So, what's everyone's doing today?"

Ramón gives Dad a funny look. We're punished, so it's not like we can hang out. We're pretty much stuck in this house. The only difference is the chores. Yesterday we cleaned up the garage. Ramón and I sweated our lives away going through storage bins and throwing things out. Who knew this family could accumulate so much junk?

Mom enters the dining room in her bathrobe. Dad pours her a cup of coffee and gives her a mimosa. Mom sips coffee first.

"I've got band practice," Ramón says. At least the guys will have a clean garage to practice in. As for my Sunday plans, I'll be doing what I've been doing for the past few days—sulking, being sad, wondering if Joanne is still mad at me, imagining what my synchro friends are doing. Basically, the usual.

"No plans," I say, and stare at my almost-empty plate.

"Isn't the exhibit opening today over at the Vincent Price?" Dad asks.

"Yes, there's a private opening this afternoon," Mom says. She sounds like me, not really into anything. Funny how we're both feeling miserable. I know why I'm miserable. Is her misery because I disappointed her? It probably is, and this makes me feel even more down.

"Why don't you and Nat head over to the museum together?" Dad says. "You both deserve a little break."

"Sure. That's a good idea," Mom says. "Nat, do you want to come with me?"

"I'd rather stay home," I say.

I can imagine what the event will be like. Mom will be surrounded by people she knows. She'll have these deep, long conversations, and I'll have to wait for her to finish, which she never does. I'm used to it, but I just feel naked, like I said too much when I told Mom the truth about how I feel.

"Fine," Mom says. She sounds like she's upset but is trying really hard not to show it. I feel bad, but I still don't want to go.

I take my plate to the kitchen and serve some food for Sheila. Mom and Dad keep talking. I'm glad they're not pressuring me into hanging with Mom. Mom would call it stewing, but I'm okay with allowing myself to float in this soup of sadness a little longer.

Sheila sits up in bed when I get back to my room and texts someone on her phone. I bet she's talking to Kim. I've heard her whisper into the phone when we should be sleeping.

"Here you go," I say.

"You didn't have to get this for me," Sheila says. Her eyes are still rimmed with red. I can't imagine how many tears a person can have. Sheila has already shed so many.

"Mom wants to take me out. I said no."

Sheila eats a little bit of the pancake.

"Why don't you go?" she asks.

I shrug.

"My mother has only disgust for me," she says. "Actual disgust. I tried to call her yesterday, and she hung up on me." Sheila's voice trembles. "At least your mother wants to be with you."

How can you go from birthing a child, raising her, and loving her, to hanging up on her? I've seen all those baby pictures of Sheila. Hundreds of them. Aunt Lupe loved dressing her up in the frilliest of dresses. Everything matched, even the shoes and the tiny little purses. She was like a Disney princess, right down to the perfect curls and matching ribbons. Mom never did that to me because she wanted us to dress ourselves, but I always wanted to wear everything glittery. Mom rarely bought me clothes with sequins, no matter how much I begged, so I just wore clashing colors to make up for the lack of shine. Funny how Mom allowed me to dress how I wanted to but won't let me look at fashion magazines. I guess there's a line that both Sheila and I can't cross when it comes to our own mothers.

"I'm sorry," I say.

"So am I and so will she, because I'm worth it," she says. "You're lucky, Nat."

Sheila says I'm lucky, but sometimes I don't feel that

way. This is so hard. I want to stay mad, but what good does that do? Mom's trying to figure out a way we can connect with each other again without it being awkward. Whenever I feel off, I usually force my way into a situation, headstrong, without looking around at who I'm barreling through. Maybe I need to just ease into this change, even with Mom.

"You want some orange juice? I'll be right back."

I don't wait for Sheila to answer. I just head to the kitchen. Mom and Dad are there, about to drink a second cup of coffee.

"I changed my mind. Can I go with you to the exhibit?"

"Of course. We don't have to stay long," she says. "We'll leave around one. Does that work?"

"Okay," I say. She offers me a smile and I return it, but it's like a crooked smile, not my "I love the whole world, I'm the best" smile.

I honestly don't want to go. I don't want to feel uncomfortable around my mom, but this is her way of trying to create a bridge, a bridge where we can meet. I can't burn the bridge just because I feel weird and unsteady around her.

CHAPTER 23

The Vincent Price Art Museum is one of my favorite museums in Los Angeles. I think it's because both my parents have spent so many years supporting the school where the museum is located. I know the campus very well. The museum is not super fancy, like the Los Angeles County Museum of Art, but it feels way more welcoming.

Because it's a Sunday, the museum is technically closed. This is a private event for only a select few. As soon as Mom enters the museum, everyone greets her with hugs and kisses. They greet me, too.

"You've grown so much since I saw you last!"

I know a lot of the people who are here. I've seen them at marches and community board meetings. They've fed me or looked after me while Mom or Dad gave speeches. I'm used to being around adults. It doesn't make me uncomfortable, not like it makes Joanne, who would rather hide behind a book.

I haven't texted or talked to her since the con fiasco

a week ago. Although we're in some classes together, every time I look her way, she ignores me. It's hard to go to school and see your best friend avoiding you. Ramón said to give her space, so I am. It still hurts.

There's a table of food and I go over. I need a little distance from Mom. On the drive over, we didn't really talk about anything important. She asked me about school and how I did on my math test. Nothing serious. It felt awkward.

Mom finishes greeting other guests and then searches for me.

"Do you want to look around?" she asks. She sounds so polite. We're both acting weird with each other, like we're walking on ice and afraid to fall through it.

"Okay."

The exhibit is titled *Ni santas, ni putas, solo mujeres*. I know some of the words in Spanish, but I want to make sure of their meaning, so I ask Mom to translate.

"It means we are neither saints nor whores. Simply women."

I kind of like that. It's a photography and art exhibit by Latinas. There's a large photo by the artist Laura Aguilar. It's of a woman looking at her reflection in a pool of water. The woman is big and beautiful. I can't stop staring at the image.

An entire wall is dedicated to Las Fotos Project, a group that donates cameras to young girls. I know a few girls who've been part of the program. The wall is covered with photos of girls taken by girls. There's one photo of a girl with makeup. She looks like a dancer. The picture reminds me of synchronized swimming. All that glorious, glittery eye shadow. I read the placard and see that the photographer is twelve years old, just like me. Wow.

"You like this one, too?" Mom asks.

"I guess I shouldn't, huh?" I walk away. The anger is instant, and I kind of don't regret it. I'm tired of justifying what I like when I only want to enjoy it.

"Nat, there is no need for you to be rude to me," Mom says, catching up. "I only asked you a question."

I'm on the defensive and I'm not sure how to get out of feeling this way. Mom breathes in deeply.

"You can like what you want," she says.

"Mom, let's be honest," I say. "You probably think the girls in the picture should concentrate on their homework rather than mascara."

This date is going downhill fast. I shouldn't have agreed to come.

"I'll just wait outside until you're done," I say.

I head to the entrance, but Mom stops me.

"Why are you so quick to dismiss me?" she says.

I'm at a total loss. I had no idea I had any power to dismiss anyone, especially my own mother.

"This is going to take a bit of an adjustment," she says. "I feel your dad and I have been really focused on getting our points across, on getting what we want, without paying much attention to how we go about doing that."

She pauses for what feels like forever. A person tries to get her attention. I prepare myself to be ignored, but Mom stops the woman from continuing. "Not right now. I'm having a conversation with my daughter."

This might be the first time in a long time that Mom really focuses on me. On us.

"You're right," Mom says. "This is not easy. I'm as stubborn as you are, and I've neglected to create a space where you can express yourself honestly and without fear. I'm asking you to give us a chance. To give me a chance."

This is it. This is the moment when I can stay angry or try something else. I think I need to do something different.

"I'm sorry I lied and I'm sorry I'm being rude," I say.

"And I'm sorry I've been forcing my opinions on you. Let's start over."

I give her a smile, a timid one because I feel shy. How is that even possible? Me, shy?

We both look around, a little bit lost, like we don't know what to do with our hands.

"I like that one, too."

I point to the photo by Laura Aguilar. We both walk toward the display.

"Yes, that one is a famous image. I met Laura once.

She always did such revolutionary work."

"Did?"

"Yes, she passed away a few years ago. Her work still lives, and that's important."

We continue to stare at the photo in silence.

"There are so many ways to be a Latina. So many different ways. Sometimes I think I have instructions on how," Mom says. "You know, my parents didn't believe in self-expression. They believed girls should be quiet, go to church, marry young, and not argue. I grew up in a family that instilled a lot of rules on me and Lupe about how we present ourselves. They taught us that to be a woman and a mother, you must look a certain way."

I'm too young to remember my grandparents. They passed away when I was four or five years old. There are pictures of us together, of Grandma Shorty holding me on her lap. She looks more like my aunt, and my mother looks more like her father.

"When I moved away to college and met your dad, I started discovering my voice. I also decided I didn't need makeup or tight clothes to prove anything. I was going to use my voice instead," Mom says.

We walk alongside each other, stopping to see the photos and read the accompanying captions. It's nice to see the work without so many people around. It's such a rare treat. This moment with Mom is also rare. Sure, we have our dates, but sometimes it feels like they're just obligations, her way of making sure she doesn't completely ignore me. It's not to say I'm not happy I get to see the exhibit, but how different would today have been if I had asked her to a synchronized swimming meet or a *makeup con*? An entire convention dedicated to talking about and trying on makeup. If that doesn't sound amazing, I don't know what does!

Mom gently holds my hand. I turn to face her. I know the next thing she says will be important, so I listen. Really listen.

"Nat, you're right. I've been really judgmental when it came to your love for fashion and beauty. I did the same thing to Sheila. I've imposed my beliefs on you without allowing you to make your own decisions," she says. "I can't say I won't keep doing it. I will always have an opinion, but I promise to listen to you more."

This makes me feel good. It's all I want, to be heard and not feel bad for the things I like. "Thanks, Mom."

"You're still punished for lying. You will have to make up for that."

"Yes, Mom."

She keeps holding my hand and I don't mind it at all. I love my mom. I love how she isn't one to keep her sorries to herself. I love that she's thinking about me and we're both trying to communicate with each other. Things change.

"Mom, what's going to happen with Sheila?" I ask.

She pauses.

"Well, I'm not sure. Your aunt is not allowing for much wiggle room. She's afraid, and her fear is clouding everything around her," she says. "It's hard when your own family believes in antiquated notions about sexuality. We all need to grow alongside our kids. Allow them to learn new things and change. Even me. I was so stuck in what I thought feminism should look and be instead of being more fluid in that definition. Aunt Lupe and I have a lot to learn."

I let what she says sink in. It feels okay being quiet for a few seconds.

"Sheila will stay with us for now. I know it's a big adjustment for you, having to share your bedroom. Hopefully it's temporary. We'll see."

I hope there comes a time when Sheila will stop crying. I don't know what it feels like to have a mother look at her the way my aunt looked at her when she said she was seeing Kim.

"On our next date, I want to pick the place," I say. This is a bold act. Mom's usually the one who decides where we go on our dates. But if this is supposed to be a new relationship, I want to have a say in how we shape it.

"Okay, I would like that," she says. There's a bit of nervousness behind her words. This makes me laugh. She has no idea where I'll drag her to. "But please don't take me to an MMA fight. I don't think I can stomach that."

"No, that's more a Ramón-and-Dad thing. I was thinking maybe a movie night at home, with popcorn?"

"I can handle a movie!" Little does she know, I plan to use the movie night to introduce her to Esther Williams. I'm warming her up to synchronized swimming with all its Technicolor glory. *Just you wait, Mom,* I think to myself. Maybe she'll find the beauty in it like I do. Maybe she'll see what I like about it and how it makes me feel empowered. It's a total possibility.

We see the exhibit slowly and find ourselves in front of Las Fotos Project pieces. There are pictures of girls laughing. Holding hands. Doing each other's makeup. Staring proudly at the camera. It's true. There are so many ways to be a girl.

CHAPTER 24

I read her text again. It's just. One. Word: "Okay."

It's Monday, exactly nine days since Joanne has looked at me, let alone spoken to me. Nine days is an eternity in my book. Even when I was juggling synchronized swimming and lying while still going to school, I always communicated. Even if the text was just to say "Hi, I'm still here."

When I texted her last night, asking if it was okay to meet, her only response was the one word. Nothing more. How does one person shut out their best friend? Well, I guess I can see how easily it can happen. I just have to think of Aunt Lupe, who's still living in hate, to see how it happens. Well, I don't want to live in hate. I want Joanne to be back in my life, and I won't do what Aunt Lupe is doing. I'm going to fight for this friendship because it's worth it.

Of course, if she doesn't want anything more to do with me, I have to respect that. Ramón says you can't force a person to like or love you. I was really angry when he said that. A no to me always means a challenge. I guess I have to learn how to rethink that.

I asked Joanne to meet me after school. Ramón said he'll wait to walk me home. He offered to walk Joanne home, too. We'll see.

"Hi, Joanne," I say. She has this sad expression, which makes me want to tell her a bunch of jokes. But I don't have to be the one who brings sunshine. Sometimes it's okay to just be sad.

"Hi," she says. Joanne digs into her book bag and pulls out a couple of new fashion magazines. I forgot how much I missed these babies. She hands them over to me.

"Oh, thanks! Can't wait." Man, I love the glossy feel of magazines—the Photoshop, the fabulous poses, all the beautiful clothes. I know it's not real, but I can still admire it for what it is.

I dig into my book bag and pull out a stack of anime videos. I asked Ramón to take me to this shop in Little Tokyo. I know for a fact that Joanne has never seen most of these before.

"Why did you get me these?" she asks as she goes through the stack.

"I just wanted to. It's a little something for making you miss the con," I say. "It's my way of making it up to you."

As much as I want to say more, I allow the silence to just be.

"I was so angry," she finally says.

"I know."

"I couldn't even sleep, that's how angry I was. It really is the only thing I look forward to all year. Waiting for you there while everyone else was taking pictures and having fun was the most painful thing I ever had to do," she says. "I felt so lonely."

This is horrible. I feel horrible. I want to cry.

"I'm really sorry I did that to you," I say. "I'm sorry I forced you to be a part of my terrible plan to lie to everyone. I'm sorry I hurt you."

Ramón and Sheila helped me figure out how to say what I wanted to say to Joanne. It's hard to find the right words, but I hope she understands. There's a long pause.

"I'm sorry I never have money for anything," she says. "You shouldn't have to pay my way."

"You never asked me to pay your way," I say. "I just like sharing my money."

Joanne shakes her head.

"I've been thinking a lot about that. It's not fair to you. Besides, I'm starting to get money from my family. It's not much, but it's something. I don't want to feel like I'm taking advantage of you."

Although I want to argue with Joanne, I won't. She feels this way and I have to listen to her.

"I miss us," Joanne says.

"I miss us, too."

We don't hug, because that would be straight out of

a corny TV show. Instead, we share very goofy smiles. We walk toward Ramón, who happens to be standing by Beto.

"So, what's happening with the L.A. Mermaids?" Joanne asks.

I shrug. I actually don't know. Mom and Dad will be having a discussion with me about the team and whether or not I'll be allowed back. There's no need for a PowerPoint presentation. We're just going to go over the finances and talk truthfully about the pros and cons.

"They're going to decide later today. Who knows? It could go either way," I say. "Want to come over later this week to watch those?" I point at the videos she's holding.

Popcorn. Magazines. Manga. I'm so glad Joanne said yes.

"Hey, Nat, I bet you can't drink this whole bottle of Coke faster than me." Beto is running his mouth again.

It's been how many months since I beat him at the pool, and he's still thinking about it. Joanne and I look at each other and laugh. How sad is Beto? Doesn't he know once you're beaten, there's no turning back? This isn't like boxing, where there's always a rematch.

"Here's the thing, Beto, I'm only looking toward the future. The past is the past," I say. "And you, Beto, are the past."

Beto's cheeks are drooping. Ramón just shakes his head, a smirk emerging from his face.

I place my arm around Joanne's shoulders and we walk past them.

"You wish you could be us, Beto." I say this at the top of my lungs for no reason. Joanne and I laugh and laugh.

CHAPTER 25

~~~~~~~~

A month later

There are only two teams ahead of us. Only two. I recognize a couple of the girls from earlier competitions. After a while, you see familiar faces. Coach Yvette says when you compete for years, you end up making friends with your rivals. It's not a big deal.

This is the first competition being held at Exposition Park pool. I now understand what home-court advantage means. I feel way more confident because I know this pool. This is the place I practice every week. But just because this is our pool, it doesn't mean we're the winners. It means our team has to be the host. The parents on our team have volunteered to work the concession stand.

"Good luck," I say to the team in front of me.

Ayana gives me a scowl. "Seriously?" she says.

"Maybe what Nat is doing right here is actually like a reverse good luck," Daniel says. "By wishing them good

221

luck, what she's really doing is hoping they forget their whole routine."

"I mean good luck," I say. "If by chance they happen to forget the beat of their song, then it's not my fault."

"I don't like this new Nat," Mayra says. "I'm not sure it's actually her. She's probably possessed."

They continue to tease me. Jeez. I give one person a compliment and the world turns upside down. They don't get it. I'm an evolving person.

Mom and Dad decided to let me go back on the team after speaking with Coach Renée and Coach Yvette. Mom is still very much against the "water pageant," but she likes the team. I knew she would, once she got to see us in action.

One thing she didn't like was when I told her about the private event I did. She was so mad. I am never to do that again. It's fine by me. I don't think Mayra will ask me to, anyway.

"Do you need anything? Your towel? A drink?"

Ayana's mom will not quit. I want to laugh, but I won't. If her mother ever stopped, Ayana would probably throw a big party to celebrate.

"Please, Mom, go to your seat," she says. "You're going to get us disqualified."

Mrs. Fekadu runs back to the bleachers. She's sitting not too far from my family. There's Ramón, bobbing his head to the music. I can see Mom in the audience.

She's sharing food with Dad. It looks like a taco from the food truck. Joanne is beside them. She holds the latest manga, but she's not really reading it. Not now, anyway. She waves, and I smile at her.

We're about to begin.

Yes, we are dancing to the same song since we first started learning about tucks and lifts and sculls. Yes, it's the exact same routine. We've practiced it hundreds of times. It doesn't matter. When we walk on deck, in unison, something magical happens. The butterflies in my stomach start to rev up, but not in a horrible, impending-doom way. My focus slowly turns to my teammates and how we become one person. It's so strange but true.

The music begins, and we dive in.

I avoid a kick from Ayana just in time to grab Mayra's foot to help lift her up. Mayra is the flyer, so it's on us—Ayana, Olivia, Daniel, and me—to grab her feet to boost her straight up above the surface. When we started practicing our lifts, I had a chance to be the flyer, too. I felt very Esther Williams. All that was needed to complete my water fantasy were fireworks and hundreds of girls swimming in a circle around me. And lots of makeup, of course.

Usually, the swimmers who get lifted up in the air are the smallest on the team. That's what happens in most of the synchronized swimming competitions I've seen. Well, I spoke to both Coach Yvette and Coach Renée.

Why do we have to do the same thing? Why can't I be the one getting lifted? Sure, the work is way harder on my teammates. There's no doubt about that. But how amazing would it be for the team as a whole? For the audience to see someone like me, a beautiful fat girl, taking center stage? I think it would be really cool.

Coach Renée said I was right. I'm not be the one being lifted today, but I will be in the next competition, and I'm so excited.

We're up to the best part. The part when everyone can see our faces while we do our quick arm movements. When we raise our hands and flick our wrists. Giving a little attitude. Always with a big smile. I love this. I can hear the cheering, too. Everyone is clapping. The butterflies are soaring now, and it's the best feeling.

We end at exactly the right time. A perfect routine!

"Thank you, L.A. Mermaids!"

The announcer says each of our names, and when he does, we lift our bodies a bit out of the water and give a wave. I wave to my parents, who are standing up and shouting my name. I knew Mom would love our routine. I just knew it.

"That was awesome!" I say once we are all out of the pool.

"I forgot one of the counts," Daniel says.

"So did I, but who cares?" I say. "Hopefully the judges didn't notice."

"We nailed the lift, though," Olivia says.

"Yeah, we did!"

"I know!" Ayana says.

We hug each other, celebrating like we're the best thing in the whole wide world. You would think we just competed at the Olympics. We act like we got first place. It's kind of ridiculous and great.

"Mermaids, there are other teams about to perform. Show some respect."

One of the judges reprimands us, and we shape up real quick with apologies. We walk over to our tent and celebrate some more.

"Congrats!" Mom pokes her head into the tent. Because we're done with our routine, we can finally eat. After that demanding routine, I'm famished. Mom hands me a couple of tacos.

"That was incredible, Nat!" she says. "You were all incredible!"

Sheila is here, too. They walk over and Kim gives me a hug, but her T-shirt gets drenched because I'm still wet. I feel bad, but it's kind of funny, too.

An alarm goes off and I search my bag to shut off my phone. It's time for my breathing exercises. Although the meditation app is still too hard to follow, I set an alarm to remind myself to do my breathing exercises throughout the day. Plus, Mom signed us both up for a meditation class. She told me about her anxiety. Mom said when she was young, if she had a book report to do, she would get so nervous, her body would get covered in hives. Now, that's anxiety. I have not had that happen to me, but I can totally relate.

We start our meditation class next week. It's every Tuesday after school. She'll pick me up and take me there so we can do this thing together. I'm kind of excited about it.

"Gather around for the awards."

I pull on my team jacket before heading over. Mom bought it for me just in time for this competition. When she asked me to open the just-delivered box and I saw it was the jacket, I let out a really loud squeal. It felt like Christmas!

Ayana sits next to me, as does Daniel. Olivia and Mayra are right by us. Our coaches want us to keep our makeup on for group photos afterward and I'm okay with it, although Mom isn't too happy. She's slowly getting used to my synchro-swimming life, although she still questions things. It's a process, is what Mom likes to say.

Throughout the competitions I've attended, there has always been one team that has stood out: the Santa Monica Sirens. When they perform, they rarely make a mistake. They're practically perfect. Daniel told me they practice every day. I guess if we could practice every day, we would be winning medals, too. I don't know. I think their routine today was a little stiff, but that's just me.

Our age category is up. Daniel holds my hand. I take Ayana's hand. Ayana holds Mayra's, and Olivia takes Daniel's other one. Everyone is sort of holding their breath. I definitely am as we wait for the announcer to call out the winners.

"In fourth place, the La Mirada Aquamaids!"

Okay, we didn't make it to fourth place, so maybe there's a chance we can place third. Daniel squeezes my hand so tight, I think it's going numb. I've got to remember to breathe!

"In third place, the Santa Clara Aquabelles!"

Oh no. Were we that bad? We didn't even place third. I look over to my team and everyone has the same face I have. I'm almost a hundred percent sure we only made a couple of mistakes on our routine. Am I wrong?

"Hold on, everyone. There are still a lot more awards to give," the announcer says over the cheering crowd. Time totally stands still. My heart is about to burst out of my chest if the announcer doesn't give us the news already.

"In second place, the L.A. Mermaids!"

We jump up and down and scream! I can't believe it! We got second place! We walk up to the podium with such glee. I am about to explode with happiness. Each one of us gets a medal placed around our neck. When I go up for mine, the woman says, "Congratulations," and I say,

"Thank you!" Well, I kind of yell it. I'm so happy.

We stand there and wait for the Santa Monica Sirens to claim their first-place win.

"Congratulations." I turn to them while they hold their trophies in their hands. "But watch out. We're coming for you and that first-place trophy."

The girls on the team laugh nervously. They don't know how to react. We will definitely beat them. I know it. I can feel it in my bones.

We grin and pose for a hundred million photos. Mom is right there along with all the other parents and friends taking pictures with her camera. Dad gives me a thumbs-up and I can't stop smiling. Funny how things have changed. It was only a few months ago when I got kicked out of a pool for gambling and arguing with haters. Now I'm meditating and taking pictures like a celebrity. I love it!

Because it's our pool, we decide to fool around in the water. We only have thirty minutes before we have to leave, but it's more than enough time.

"I bet you I can eggbeat way longer than you can."

Ayana rolls her eyes. Daniel, on the other hand, is willing to prove me wrong. He's a total sucker because if there's anything I know, I always play to win.

"Okay, five bucks says I can beat you," I say.

"I thought you said you're not allowed to bet," Ayana says.

"You're right," I say. "Okay, let's compete for bragging rights and a taco."

"Okay, a taco."

"Let's do it."

Mayra and Olivia can't decide who to root for. After all these months practicing together, I would think this would be a total no-brainer. Obviously, I'm going to win.

"On your mark," Ayana says.

Joanne watches from the bleachers, smiling. She knows what's up.

"Get set!"

"You are so going down, Nat," Daniel says.

Bad-mouthing me? I don't think so.

"Go!"

"I'm going to eggbeat until eternity!" I yell.

There's no doubt, I can do this forever.

ACKNOWLEDGMENTS

In 2016, a young swimming instructor at a Los Angeles city public pool asked my then-seven-year-old daughter Isabelle if she wanted to learn how to dance in the water. Thus began our ten-year journey with synchronized (now artistic) swimming and with the team L.A. Aquanymphs, founded by Patrice Rice. I spent so many hours traveling all over watching these beautiful brown and Black kids being fearless and powerful. They're my inspiration for *Barely Floating*. This book is also dedicated to the tireless public city pool workers helping to keep these much-needed facilities opened. They practically raised my kids, and I'm sure I'm not the only one.

Thank you to my amazing editor, Namrata Tripathi, and the rest of the Kokila team for giving this middle grade novel so much love and attention. Thank you to the talented Boricua artist Ericka Lugo and cover designer Kelley Brady. The cover brings me so much joy! And as always, thanks to my agent, Eddie Schneider. It's hard to believe this is our eighth novel together!

Finally, I'm so lucky I still get to share these stories with you, the readers! Thank you!